She'd kissed him. He'd kissed her back. And he'd blown her socks off.

Margot got to the kitchen, and when she knew Daniel couldn't see her, she slumped against the counter.

What shocked her almost as much was the way she was with him. Good Lord, she was a femme fatale, a siren, a vamp. And sexy? She'd go to bed with herself, she was so damned seductive.

Her heart still raced, her legs wobbled and she could hardly see straight. All this from a guy she barely knew, who had all the style of a stalk of broccoli and who blushed at the drop of a double entendre.

But the truth of it was, despite this moment of reflection, she felt like a goddess. Oz, the great and powerful. It was unbelievable, unprecedented.

And so, so excellent.

Dear Reader,

Oh, was this book a blast to write! I haven't had such a good time in...well, a long time. Daniel was such a sweetie pie, but I'll tell you the truth—he took me completely by surprise when he and Margot did the wild thing. I expected him to be a nice guy, maybe a little shy. Boy, was I wrong. Not that he wasn't nice. But shy? Not even close. As for Margot, I think she might be closer to me than any heroine I've ever written. So full of contradictions! Wanting so badly to make the right choice, but how can she when she doesn't know what the right choice is?

Yep, just like real life. Just like me.

I hope you find a little of you in Margot, and that you, too, fall in love with Daniel. I sure did.

Be good...but not too good!

Jo Leigh

Books by Jo Leigh

HARLEQUIN BLAZE

Don't miss any of our special offers. Write to us at the following address for information on our newest releases.

Harlequin Reader Service
U.S.: 3010 Walden Ave., P.O. Box 1325, Buffalo, NY 14269
Canadian: P.O. Box 609, Fort Erie, Ont. L2A 5X3

A LICK AND A PROMISE

Jo Leigh

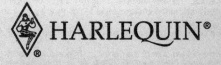

HARLEQUIN®

TORONTO • NEW YORK • LONDON
AMSTERDAM • PARIS • SYDNEY • HAMBURG
STOCKHOLM • ATHENS • TOKYO • MILAN • MADRID
PRAGUE • WARSAW • BUDAPEST • AUCKLAND

To my beautiful, incredible niece Rachel, with all my love.

ISBN 0-373-79169-0

A LICK AND A PROMISE

Copyright © 2005 by Jolie Kramer.

This edition published by arrangement with Harlequin Books S.A.

www.eHarlequin.com

Printed in U.S.A.

_1_

THE LETTUCE SUCKED. Great. Marvelous. Just the way she wanted her first day as the food stylist for Whompies to start off. Yeah, that's Whompies. Of the double double Angus beef Whompie burger with the special curly fries. Of course, she didn't really work for Whompies, she worked for Galloway and Donnelly, one of the top advertising agencies in Manhattan. Who, if they liked the work she did on this shoot, could very well put her on staff, which would be, in the words of her aunt Sadie, such a blessing! Galloway and Donnelly's food division paid top dollar, and got the best gigs.

On her own, she'd landed some pretty good jobs. That one for _Bon Appétit_ had been stellar. But working for G and D would put her on the map. After five, six years working with some of the best foodies on the planet, she, Margot Janowitz, would have the name recognition and contacts to go back out on her own. Then she could ask for the moon…and get it.

But first, she had to get some lettuce that didn't look like roadkill, pronto. She got her work phone book out of her kit and headed back to the prep kitchen, almost tripping over the thick cables connected to the mega-huge lights in Stage Four, one of the MidTown Production's sound stages used for making commercials and rock videos.

She was going to be here a lot in the next five months. Not continuously, of course. In between the Whompies shoots she'd have print gigs, but it was the TV commercials that she was most excited about. Making burgers, fries, milk shakes, sodas, pizza, onion rings look so deliciously scrumptious that people watching the commercials would leap off their couches and race over to Whompies to chow down on everything on the menu.

Inside the huge prep kitchen, two of the camera guys were eating take-out Chinese broccoli beef. They both had their feet up on the big white table, having shoved her notebook to the very edge. She snatched it up, trying not to freak. Very calmly, she looked at the two men, both in their early twenties, and said, "Do you know what this table is?"

One of them, the light-haired guy who had clearly forgotten that hair needed washing from time to time, looked up with a full mouth, and replied, "Huh?"

"I said, do you know what this table is?"

He shook his head while he swallowed.

"It's a food preparation table. Where actual food is prepared. And mostly, we don't like it smelling of feet."

The blond guy grunted. But they both slid their feet to the ground. They didn't stop eating.

Margot sighed. "Shoo. Scram. Leave." She waved four fingers. "Bu-bye."

The darker guy stood. He wore cargo pants a couple of sizes too big, a Third Eye Blind T-shirt and a Mets cap. He raised his right eyebrow in her direction, then shuffled out, heading toward the employee lounge, where they should have been in the first place. Blondie followed. Slowly. But finally, she was alone.

It was just past 5:30 a.m. and she wanted all the food prep to be done before eight. The rest of the staff, whom she hadn't met, would be here soon. From her past experience assisting on other food commercials, there would be at least one more stylist and three or four assistants. Which would be great, All she had to do was get fresh, crisp lettuce. Simple. Easy. She had a mile-long list of suppliers. No reason at all for her heart to beat like a Led Zeppelin drum solo.

She stopped. Took a deep breath. This was just like the dozens and dozens of jobs she'd assisted on. The only difference was, on this one, she was in charge. Which was a good thing. A marvelous thing. Something she'd worked hard for.

From this moment forward, this job was going to be one triumph after another. On time, on budget, exactly to the Whompies specifications. Period. She knew what to do, knew how to do it. Piece of cake.

She went back into the main studio, where more folks had arrived. She didn't know anyone. Not yet. But soon, they'd all be joking around together, bitching about the work, pulling out all the stops to make the product shine.

She loved this part. A lot. The whole team thing. That was the bonus of doing television. It was good on print shoots, but this was more. Bigger. Better.

Her phone vibrated in her apron pocket. She flipped it on, her earphone snugly in place, as it always was. "Margot."

"Babycakes."

Margot smiled at her neighbor's voice as she went to the craft service table to get her coffee. "Hi, Devon. 'Sup?"

"Just checking in on your first day at the new gig."

"Well, except for phone calls at dawn, things are going really well."

She heard a ferocious yawn. Then, "I'm going to bed in five. You know, the new guy is moving in today."

"Did you find out anything else?"

Her neighbor chuckled. "Eric thinks he's straight."

Margot checked out the few people standing around the doughnuts. She didn't recognize any of them. "Gotta love Eric," she said.

"He's never wrong. He also said he's a major babe, although he was wearing off-the-rack."

"I'm surprised he wasn't struck by lightning."

Devon laughed. "I'm too tired to live. Kick ass, babe. We'll talk tomorrow."

She clicked off her phone, then it was her turn at the coffee. She should have brought a mug; she hated foam cups. Behind her, some grips and electricians were talking and laughing, and she got excited all over again at the thought of soon becoming one of the gang. In fact, she was going to introduce herself to the woman behind her, then her phone rang again.

"Margot."

"Hello, darling."

"Ma."

"I didn't wake you, did I?"

"Nope. Been up since three-thirty."

"That's not good. You're not sleeping?"

"New job. Remember?"

"Of course I do. That's why I'm calling. To wish you luck."

"That's nice, Ma. Really. But I'm in the middle—"

"Would you do something for me?"

Margot sighed. Getting off the phone with her mother should be an Olympic event. "What?"

"Talk to him."

"Him" was her father. It was always her father. Unless it was one of her uncles. Or her cousins. Or her neighbors. "What's wrong?"

"He bought five cases of broken dishes."

Margot sighed. "Are you sure they're all broken?"

"If they aren't, they will be by the time he gets them. I ask you. What is he going to do with five cases?"

"I don't know, Mom, but I'm sure he has his reasons."

"Reasons. We have the *meshugge* storage unit which is costing an arm and a leg, and now he says he needs another unit because he can't move the merchandise."

"I'll talk to him. But, Ma, I have to go."

"Okay, *bubele*. We'll talk later."

It wasn't even six, and the troops were calling already. She fully expected to hear from Corrie, her other next-door neighbor, before seven. Which was fine.

Margot liked keeping in touch, and her co-op in Chelsea was a hotbed of wonderfulness, full of fascinating characters who she'd come to love. A month ago Seth Boronski had died, poor man, leaving his second-floor unit vacant, and just last week it had been bought by a single man. Daniel was his name, but that's all Margot knew about him. Which was unusual, because frankly, no one knew more about the comings and goings of 18 West 16th Street. Not even the super, who only came around when threatened by mass revolt or bribed with oatmeal raisin cookies.

The new job had been all she'd thought about for days, planning, thinking, styling in her head. She'd have time to scope out Daniel on Sunday during the weekly co-op dinner.

Right now, though, she needed to get to the kitchen. She had to order the lettuce. And the troops should be arriving any minute.

DANIEL WINCED as his friends Terry and Bill lurched through the front door with his oak headboard, narrowly missing the molding. "Careful with that, damn it."

Bill gave him an evil look. "You know what you can do with your careful, Daniel, old buddy?"

"That headboard's eighteenth century."

Terry cut the discussion short with a succinct curse.

"Fine. Be asses," Daniel said, leading them into the bedroom. "Put it there."

The two men, his old roommates from Rutgers, put the headboard down with matching grunts. "Think you could get some heavier furniture next time?" Bill asked.

"I'll work on it," Daniel said, anxious to get back to the truck. Steve was down there, guarding the rest of his possessions, although the lion's share of boxes was already inside. He had beer in the fridge and pizzas coming in an hour, so he wanted to be done by then. "Come on, we still have the rest of the bed."

Terry, who was a big guy in college and an even bigger guy now that he was a stockbroker, wiped his face with his NYT T-shirt. "I can't believe you got me here to do this on a Thursday. I'm losing millions and sweating way the hell too much."

"It's your vacation, and I don't recall a lot of arm-twisting," Daniel said as he led his reluctant mover toward the door.

"Some vacation. I should be in Aruba, soaking in the sun."

"What about me?" Bill said. "I'm not on vacation."

"You're on a permanent vacation," Terry said, shouldering his friend out of his way. "In case you've forgotten."

"Hey, I offered to pay for movers."

Daniel laughed. "That's what I like about you, Bill. When in doubt, throw money around."

Bill shrugged. He still had his good looks, although his lifestyle was starting to show on his face. The heir to a huge manufacturing fortune, he'd given the reins of the business to his younger brothers and decided on a life of decadence. But he was such a generous guy, none of his friends could complain too much. Still, Daniel worried about Bill's fast-lane life. The man was pushing thirty-five and the way he was going, it was questionable he'd reach forty.

They got to the elevator, and rested against the walls as they rode down the two floors. They'd started out taking the stairs, but exhaustion had hit hard about two hours ago. Daniel still couldn't believe he'd done it. Given up his place in Greenwich, Connecticut, to move to the city. The short commute alone was worth it, but that he'd found this place in Chelsea, well, that was something else.

Chelsea. Everyone knew about Chelsea. How the art scene had changed the landscape in the late eighties and expatriates fleeing the Village's high prices had moved here, renovating lofts and garment buildings into high-end co-ops. The area had been predominantly gay, but now was home for an eclectic mix of people. That mix gave Chelsea a vibrancy, an aliveness, and had attracted him. In Greenwich, he'd had a nice place, but there was no… Hell, he didn't know what was missing, except that his life had become stale. Boring as an old shoe.

His move had raised eyebrows at the firm, but he didn't care. Well, he cared, but not enough to alter his plans.

They reached the lobby and headed for the double-parked truck in front of the building. Steve rested against the back bumper, reading. He held up a finger, making them wait while he finished his chapter, then closed the paperback. "Bed?"

"Yeah," Daniel said. "And it's your turn, so get off your lazy butt."

Steve looked at the other two men. "Can you believe this guy?"

"I say we let him take up the mattress by himself," Bill said, jumping up to sit next to Steve.

"Hey, I've got pizza coming in an hour. I'd prefer to eat it hot."

Terry squished up his face and repeated Daniel's words in a voice worthy of a cranky two-year-old.

Daniel ignored him, jumped up onto the back of the

truck and whipped the guys into shape. Bill stayed behind this time, but they managed to get the mattress upstairs without him. Waiting just inside the door was a surprise. A woman stood amidst the jumble, tall, very thin, wearing a tiny stretch top that just covered her small, high breasts, and tights. Her abdomen was bared, and he could tell she worked out.

"Hi," she said, giving him a wide smile. "Welcome to the building. I'm Corrie. 302. Married to Nels."

"I'm Daniel." He held out his hand. "Daniel Houghton III."

She put her little birdlike hand in his, and he was careful not to squeeze too hard. "Sundays we have this dinner," she said. Her voice was high and as thin as she was. "Everybody comes. We go from apartment to apartment. We all make something. Appetizers, salads, main course." She blushed. It made her look like a teenager. "Anyway, first time, you're off the hook for food. But please join us, okay?"

He nodded. "I'd love to."

She smiled again. "I've got—" she nodded toward the door "—things to do."

"Thanks, Corrie," he said.

"We start at five," she said, backing up, almost tripping over a box. "Oh, you can bring wine. Wine's good."

"Great."

Behind him, the guys came out of the bedroom.

"Okay, then," she said. "Bye."

"Bye."

"Now I get it," Terry said.

Daniel turned. "Get what?"

"Why you moved here. All these straight women have so few straight guys to choose from." He turned to Steve. "He's not as dumb as he looks."

"Well, thanks. Now get your ass back to the truck."

Steve laughed as he headed out the door. Terry just glared. But they'd finish the job soon, and Daniel was grateful for that. He had four days to unpack this mess. Then it was back to work.

He was an architect. A good one. The firm he worked for, Kogen, Teasdale and Webster, was well respected in the industry, and he was inching his way up, slowly but surely, to partner.

Daniel checked his watch. He figured another three hours and he'd be alone. Not that he didn't appreciate his friends lending a hand, but he wanted to get on with it. Get this place livable so he could begin this new phase of his life. Exploring the streets, checking out the architecture, the galleries, restaurants, finding his local market, the dry cleaners.

He grinned. Dinner with all the tenants. In the five years he'd lived in Greenwich, he'd met two of his neighbors, but he'd never shared so much as a cup of coffee with them. This was a good move. A new beginning. But he'd have to break out of his old habits, be willing to experiment. He headed toward the elevator. This felt right. Just what he needed. He hoped.

"OH, MY GOD, he's the cutest thing you've ever seen. I swear, Margot, he's like six feet tall, and he has dark hair that's tragically unhip, and he wears these round glasses that went out with the eighties, and his jeans were ironed. He tucked in his Polo shirt, for heaven's sake. And I swear, if I wasn't married I'd eat him up with a spoon. Wait'll you see."

Margot couldn't help but laugh. When Corrie got going it was like listening to an auctioneer on helium. "Is he coming on Sunday?"

"Yep. He's in. Oh, God, what a doll baby. I'm telling you, girl, we're going to have so much fun with this one."

"It sounds like a major redo."

"From the ground up. His tennis shoes. Did I mention his tennis shoes?"

"No, but I can't hear about it now. I've got serious staff issues."

"Oh, I'm such a jerk. You're having this first-day thing, and I'm going on and on about Daniel. Can you stand it? Daniel Houghton III. Have you ever?"

"Never. But they only gave me two assistants, which is insanity. I'll talk to you later."

"Break a leg."

"Right. Bye." Margot switched off her phone and watched as one of the assistants, Bettina, shaved lettuce. The other one, Rick, was sorting buns. She couldn't believe there were only two, and neither one of them had enough experience to clean the fridge.

It was unheard of that there were so few people on a food commercial. She'd put in a call to her boss, Janice, but the woman hadn't been there. Surely this was a mistake, and would be rectified soon, but in the meantime, she had to get her ass in gear if she expected to get anything out to the director.

They had almost a hundred buns that had to be sorted,

looking for the perfect combination of symmetry, color, shape, size and the placement of the sesame seeds. Once they'd found the perfect bun, what they called the *hero* in the biz, they'd set that aside. The second best, they'd use as the stand-in, building a burger for the lighting guys. She had her bag of extra sesame seeds in her kit, along with glue, in case they had to make adjustments.

Then there was the lettuce to tear, the ketchup to drain, the burgers to shape and cook just enough so they wouldn't look raw, the grill marks to place, the cheese to melt, the onions, the tomatoes… It was too much for so few people with so little time.

She sat down with Rick and examined buns. The thing to do was take it one step at a time. And not hyperventilate.

Fifteen minutes and forty-six rejects later, the assistant director stuck her head in the door. "What's your ETA?"

"At least three hours."

"Oh, shit."

"It's the best I can do."

"I'll tell him."

Him was Joe DeVario, the director. In the five seconds she'd talked to him, she'd gotten a really bad feeling. He scowled, didn't shake her hand and dismissed her without so much as a backward glance.

Her mood didn't improve when she heard his voice, yelling from the sound stage.

Not a good way to start a new job.

The only bright spot in all of this was one Daniel Houghton III. Interesting.

From Corrie's description, he sounded like a man who needed a fashionista's touch. A designer's eye.

Devon and Eric had to be giddy with anticipation. She just hoped they wouldn't scare Daniel off, as they had one of the previous residents.

Margot smiled. There was nothing she liked more than a new project. A challenge. Surprises.

"Aha," she said, holding up the most gorgeous bun this side of heaven. "We have our hero!"

2

DANIEL LOOKED at the clothes in his closet as he tucked his white towel around his waist. He had no idea what to wear to this Sunday-night dinner. He'd only had glimpses of his neighbors in the four days he'd lived here. Mostly he'd been buried in unpacking, and although he wasn't quite finished, he'd gotten most of it done.

He gazed around his new bedroom. His furniture looked good against the white walls, his favorite books placed neatly in the shelves. He'd even splurged and bought a new tartan bedspread with pillow shams, something he'd never had before. But this was his new beginning, and there was no law that said he had to have a traditional quilt just because he'd always had one. He could do whatever he pleased. Go nuts. Buy art because he liked it, not just because it would be a good investment.

Starting tomorrow, he'd go back to his regular world, but he had the feeling it wouldn't be the same. Stepping outside of his comfort zone had already changed him in ways he hadn't anticipated. Last night, for dinner, he'd ordered a Hawaiian pizza. He'd hated it, but that was beside the point.

Back to the wardrobe. Nothing seemed right. Not his

jeans, not his suits. Finally, he settled on something simple. Black slacks, white shirt, gray sportjacket. And what the hell, the purple tie his niece had given him last Christmas.

The decision made, he went back to the bathroom to finish getting ready. As he shaved, he studied himself in the mirror, not at all happy with how long his hair had gotten. He'd visit the barber next week. But he was pleased with the bathroom itself. A place for everything and everything in its place.

As the seconds ticked by, he grew more and more concerned about the evening's activities. Yes, he wanted to meet his neighbors, but did he really want to spend a whole night with all those strangers? Maybe he should wait, meet a few of them at a time, ease himself in instead of diving into the deep end. He'd bought wine. Maybe he should go up, give them the wine, then come up with some excuse why he couldn't stay.

That sounded right. He'd have a quick look at who he would be dealing with, then he'd be better prepared for future encounters.

He wiped the last of the shaving cream off his face and neck, then headed to the bedroom. It was almost five, and he wanted to be on time.

"MY BASIL IS DEAD."

"Oh, no. When are the services?"

Margot flipped her hair back with her free hand and adjusted the volume on her phone. "You're a riot, Corrie, and you should immediately go on the road with your act."

"Only you, Margot, my dear, can tell a person to go jump in a lake in such an endearing fashion."

"I must get fresh basil, or the entire meal is going to be dog chow. So come early and let everyone in."

"They have basil at Martini's."

"They have lousy basil at Martini's. I'm going to the Garden of Eden."

"You've got to be kidding."

Margot looked at the ingredients for her grilled pizzas. Everything was ready, the dough was sufficiently rested, the coals in the grill on her patio were already lit. She'd have to cab it to the Garden, but their produce was the best, and it was worth it. She reminisced with longing about when she lived next door to her parents' grocery store, where everything needed for any meal was footsteps away. But she'd spent years scoping out the best of the best food sources in Chelsea and beyond, and most of the friendly purveyors delivered. If there was enough time. "I'll be back before you know it."

"But Daniel is coming."

"Tell him to just breathe hard until I get back."

Corrie sighed, but Margot could tell she was smiling. "Fine. Be late to your own party."

"It's just us guys," Margot said, grabbing her pocketbook as she headed for the door. "There's wine in the fridge."

"Hurry."

"Yes, dear." Margot clicked off her phone, and dashed out, hoping like hell she could quickly catch a cab. She was actually a little nervous about tonight. She still hadn't seen Daniel, but boy, those in the know, Corrie, Devon, Eric, had drooled over his potential.

As a group, they had more in common with *Queer Eye for the Straight Guy* than they should. They loved nothing better than sitting in the local eateries and dishing on the clientele, and how to revamp them. Unfortunately, they rarely got to use their considerable skills with real-life people. Only twice, actually, and Tad didn't count. One shopping trip with Devon and Eric had been enough to send him scampering to Yonkers on the first train. So Daniel was a treat indeed.

She ignored the elevator and raced down the stairs, ending up on the street in half the time. And as luck would have it there was a Yellow Cab, right there, and she flopped into the back seat with her heart still racing.

"Garden of Eden on 7th."

The cabbie took off, and Margot closed her eyes. Despite the excitement of Daniel, her thoughts were never far from work these days. She'd made it through Thursday and Friday, and she was pretty sure she could handle Monday. She still couldn't believe they hadn't given her more staff. It was insane trying to do everything she had to with only Bettina and Rick. They were nice enough, but she'd had to show them every step, every trick. Whompies was a major chain, and she couldn't believe there wasn't money in the budget for more stylists. But when she'd talked to Janice, her boss had strongly implied that if Margot couldn't make it work with what she had, perhaps she wasn't the right person for the job. It made her so crazy—

No. Today she would stop obsessing about work and

focus on Daniel. She was dying to see him. God, she hoped he wasn't a total stick-in-the-mud, because that would ruin everything. Although, when it came to persuasion of the personal kind, she was pretty much a tank, rolling over all obstacles in her way, whatever or whoever she had to squish.

The cab turned onto 7th, and she dug her money out of her purse. If only she could be as assertive in her work as she was with her friends. When it came to being a food stylist, she was hell on wheels. But negotiating? Playing well with others?

Oh, well. She'd continue to strive. Take baby steps until she could stride with pride. And pray she didn't self-destruct.

It was time to buy basil. And maybe some more fresh flowers. Oh, and some marinated olives. It was almost five, she'd better jet.

THE KNOCK ON THE DOOR surprised Daniel as he was on his way to get the wine from the kitchen. Corrie was there, only this time she was wearing this long pale dress that flowed over her tall, slim frame. Her hair was short and spiky, and she'd made her eyes up with quite a bit of dramatic black. Next to her was a man taller than she, dressed in a Hawaiian shirt and khaki pants. He looked as if he'd stepped out of a shampoo commercial.

"Daniel, hi. This is Devon," Corrie said.

Daniel put out his hand. "Nice to meet you. Corrie mentioned you when we met."

Devon gave her an odd look, and she seemed equally puzzled.

"Oh, no. This isn't Nels. My husband. Who can't come tonight. This is Devon. He lives on the other side of Margot. With Eric."

"Ah," Daniel said.

"We're here to get you," Corrie said, looking past him into his apartment. "Wow, it looks great."

He stepped to the side. "Come in."

"We can't stay long," she said as she checked out the room as if she wanted to redecorate. "Margot's getting basil so I have to be the hostess until she gets back."

"Margot?"

"She's first tonight. I think she's making grilled pizza."

Devon breezed by him, heading straight for the bookcases. He eyed them slowly, row by row, nodding his approval. "Interesting stuff. Lots of architecture."

"That's what I do."

Devon grunted, and Daniel wasn't sure if it was in approval or something else. Given what these two had on, he should really go change into something more casual.

"Come, come. Hurry. There's going to be pouting people in the hallways if I don't let them in."

"I—"

Devon hooked an arm around his shoulder, which wasn't a big deal, really. "Come on, New Guy. Into the fray."

"Wine."

"Ah, it's not time to whine yet," Devon said, leading him toward the door. "That's for after you meet the others."

"Um, no. I have some wine."

"Oh." The tall man let him go. "We must have vino."

"Then I'll go, uh, get it."

"That'd be good." Devon smiled, a little too kindly, as if Daniel was feebleminded.

He went to the kitchen, pulled out two bottles, one an excellent merlot, the other a decent chardonnay. When he got back to the living room, Corrie was gone, the door was open and Devon waited.

Walking as casually as he could, he closed his door behind him, silently rehearsing his speech about how he couldn't stay long.

HE WANTED MORE WINE. Lots more wine. Because he needed to be drunk to process this…menagerie.

Corrie was the normal one, and it turned out she was an ex-exotic dancer who'd had to give up her career after she'd broken her leg.

Devon was a bartender at something called a she-been, and his partner, Eric, was a chiropractor who believed in auras and spirit guides. Then there was Anya, whom Daniel guessed was in her seventies. She'd had several long, involved conversations with her pets—three poodles, two cats and a parakeet. Her best friend was Rocco, also in his golden years. He was an ex-boxer, and his whole face, not just his ears, looked like a bruised cauliflower. Rocco watched soap operas, and he knitted. Evidently, he knitted a lot, and all the tenants in the building were recipients of his largesse. Daniel kept trying to take off the floppy yellow cap, and Devon kept putting it back on his head.

The introductions were over now, and all anyone could talk about was the missing hostess. Margot. He'd already learned she was a food stylist. He'd heard of the profession, although he'd never met anyone in the trade. It made him wonder about the market for such a thing. Was the pay very good? By the look of her rather extravagantly decorated apartment, it must be.

Anyway, she was young, talented, witty, bright… going places. He'd love her. Every one of them assured him of that. He wasn't so sure. But, he had to admit, he was curious.

Just as Corrie came by to fill his glass, the front door swung open and a woman breezed in. To a chorus of applause, no less. She carried a big grocery bag, and her long dark hair billowed behind her as she crossed the room.

So this was Margot. She was taller than he'd supposed, and quite ample, although she wore a scarlet cape, so he couldn't really see much. Besides, he was too busy looking at her face to be bothered with the rest. She was…striking. A presence. Large eyes, a lush smile that made it hard not to grin in return, high cheekbones. Her hair came down past her shoulders, thick and flowing. Everything about her seemed larger than life.

"Sorry, sorry, sorry. I couldn't get a cab on 7th, and traffic was hell, but I have everything now so we can get cooking, and I hope everyone's had wine and isn't upset and oh, my God."

This she said when she stopped right in front of him. Staring, mouth open, the whole bit. Talk about knowing how to make a stranger feel welcome.

"You're…delicious."

He hadn't blushed in a long time. Not since college, at least that he could recall. But he was blushing now. Wishing like hell he'd made his excuse about five minutes ago. It wasn't too late. He could still escape before he burst into flames.

She thrust the grocery bag into Eric's hand, never once shifting her gaze from him. "I'm Margot."

"So I gathered."

In a move that would have impressed Liberace, she whipped off her cloak and tossed it behind her, directly into Corrie's waiting arms.

Now that he could see more of her, he was struck by how different she was from most of the women he knew. Miles away from those he dated, who tended to be borderline anorexic overachievers with exotic allergies. There was nothing of that in the woman in front of him. Even her dress looked like something a movie star would wear. Long, black and red, with a big glittery pin gathering the material right under her breasts. Which was what they deserved. They were impressive breasts. Bountiful was the word that came to mind.

Her laugh brought his attention back to her face. He cleared his throat, stood up. Held out his hand. "Daniel."

She looked at his hand, laughed again and shook. "Welcome to the building, Daniel."

"Thank you."

"You've met everyone?"

He nodded.

"I see Rocco made you a kicky little hat."

Oh, God. He ripped the cap off his head. "Uh, yeah."

"Don't worry. Before you know it, you'll have a scarf

and mittens to match. Come, Daniel. Let's make pizzas, shall we?"

He nodded again, only then realizing his right hand still held hers. She used the situation to pull him toward the kitchen.

It was as bright and colorful as the woman herself, with lots of knickknacks of the fifties kitsch variety. A display of PEZ dispensers was his first clue. Then there were the turquoise and pink diner accents, like the old-time malt mixer, the napkin dispenser and the pink retro stove. Even the tiles were coordinated. The only thing black in the kitchen was the Felix the Cat clock.

"You can wash the basil," she said, letting his hand go. "While I prepare the dough. Yes?"

"I'll be happy to."

She gave him another of those dazzling smiles. "Good Lord, you're Studly Do-Right. Fabulous."

If her eyes hadn't been shining like that he'd have been insulted. Maybe he was insulted anyway.

She washed her hands, dried them with a pink towel, then handed him the basil as if it were the crown jewels. It was his turn at the sink. His concentration was split between his task and Margot. She had sprinkled flour on two large pizza boards and was folding a large round of dough as if she'd done it hundreds of times.

She cut the dough in six, then brought out a wooden rolling pin and made two ovals. When she turned to the fridge, he went back to the basil, making sure it was thoroughly clean. He wrapped it in paper towels as he watched her once more.

"We're going to Corrie's next," she said. "Then Eric

and Devon's. We'll have dessert at Rocco's, which is really a treat, because he cooks a hell of a lot better than he knits."

"And you do this every Sunday?"

"Yep. These are the regulars, but the rest of the folks in the building join in from time to time. We're all pretty friendly."

"So I gathered."

She put down a large bowl filled with stuff like braided mozzarella, mushrooms, olives and tomatoes and turned to face him. "Tell me about you, Daniel."

"I'm an architect."

"Have I seen any of your work?"

"Maybe. I designed the Fourth Street library in Brooklyn Heights."

"Nope."

"Uh, the Woolsey building on lower Broadway."

She shook her head.

"Those are the biggest projects."

"Are they gorgeous?"

"Gorgeous?" He smiled. "No one's ever called them that."

"What have they called them?"

"Practical. Well built. Sturdy."

She blinked. "Tear them up."

"Pardon?"

"The basil leaves. Tear them. Into pieces." Then she turned to the pizzas and started spreading the sauce.

Devon stuck his head in the kitchen. "Hey, we're starving out here."

"Then go make sure the grill's ready."

Devon saluted. "Yes, ma'am." He did a two-point turn and marched away.

"Totally nuts, but such a sweet pea. You'll love him. And Eric. They're great."

"Have you been here long?"

"Five years. This place used to belong to my uncle Sid. He was a photographer. Mostly for *National Geographic*. Incredible life. I'll tell you about it sometime."

"Okay."

"Continue."

"What?"

"Telling me about your life."

"Ah. Well, I moved from Greenwich. Connecticut."

"Hell of a commute."

"Yeah. I got real used to the train."

She turned to him again. "Girlfriend?"

"No."

"Boyfriend?"

That took him back a step. "No."

"Ah, so you're straight."

"Are you always like this?"

"Like what? Rude?"

"I was going to say forthright."

She patted his arm. "That's sweet. Really."

He had no idea how to respond to her. How to react to this whirlwind. So he focused on the basil. He was supposed to tear it. Which he did, even though he wasn't the least bit sure he was doing it correctly.

She emptied her bowl and started slicing mozzarella so quickly it made him fear for her fingers. By the time he'd finished tearing, she had neat little bowls of accoutrements, most of which he recognized. She rubbed the crusts with olive oil, then scattered them with mozzarella, some of his basil and then some prosciutto. Then she lifted the boards, one in each hand. "Come. We grill now. Oh, and be a love and get me a glass of whatever it is you're drinking."

He nodded as he watched her walk from the kitchen. His gaze moved down the length of her, wishing he could see more of her curves. What he did see appealed in a way that surprised the hell out of him.

This Margot was something outside his ken. Brash, focused and a little nuts. But interesting. Definitely Chelsea. Completely not Greenwich.

He thought again about his excuses to leave. Now would be the perfect time. No one would think he was escaping. On the other hand, that pizza sounded really good.

3

MARGOT PLACED THE FIRST PIZZA on the grill, then the second. She stepped back, almost tripping on her little flower box, the one she was preparing for herbs. Her flowers were doing really well, but the herb thing was giving her fits. She'd tried basil, marjoram, dill, parsley and a bunch of others, but the only thing that had grown successfully was the parsley. But, she'd give it another go. Maybe get some grow lights.

Devon joined her outside, closing the sliding-glass door behind him. "So, what do you think?

She smiled. "He's yummy plus ten."

"No kidding. If I wasn't—"

"But you are."

"Very."

"And he's not."

Devon sighed. "Nope. Straight as an arrow. But you know my philosophy."

"Right. No man is truly straight. Only uneducated."

Devon lifted his highball glass. "Amen."

She looked past him to see the man in question, still wearing his jacket and tie, smiling rather confusedly at Anya. "I want to rip off his clothes—"

"Margot!"

"—and put him in some Dolce & Gabbana. Hell, even Tommy Hilfiger would be better than that getup."

Devon stood next to her, watching Daniel. "He works out."

"You think?"

"I saw him without the jacket. Yep."

"Ah, nice."

"So, you going for it?"

"Oh, yeah."

He turned, putting his free hand on her shoulder. "I meant for the whole nine yards."

"Oh."

"Come on, babycakes. This boy needs you. Look at him. He doesn't have a clue. Face it, it's destiny."

"Dev, the guy just moved in. I've talked to him for thirty seconds."

"I knew the moment I laid eyes on him. He's for you. Ready to be molded by your incredible style. He's clay, darling. Unformed. Pliable. Needy."

"Yeah, well, we'll see. I can't make a decision that momentous until I learn some things."

"Like what?"

She checked her pizzas. They were almost done. The serving platters and the cutter were at the ready. "I have no clue if the man has a sense of humor. And as we all know, that's a deal breaker."

"That's it?"

"No. He also needs to be teachable."

"He moved here from Greenwich, Connecticut. He's teachable."

"Unless he's clueless."

He turned around to face the door. "He's too delicious to dismiss out of hand. Take off those glasses, give him a decent haircut, and honey, it wouldn't matter if he couldn't tie his own shoes."

"Devon, go inside."

"Spoilsport."

She gave him a little push, and he went to join the others. Margot got busy with the pizza, transferring it onto the platter and cutting it into pieces. All the while, she kept thinking about Daniel. Devon was right. He was the most scrumptious man she'd seen in years. Totally adorable. And clearly in need of her particular talents. But would he go for it? And did she want it to be more than a makeover?

She thought about her friends online, and how she hadn't been participating with the group much since she got her new job. Eve's Apple was what they called themselves. A group of brilliant and witty women from all over the country who met in a chat room to talk about life, books, sex. Several years ago, the original founders of the group had begun something called Men To Do. The premise was that there were men out there who were completely inappropriate for the long term. Dangerous men. Foolish choices. Men you wouldn't take home to mother.

Margot had participated in every aspect of Eve's Apple, except for that last one. She'd thought about having a Man To Do, but when push came to shove, she'd never found anyone she wanted like that.

These men were for sex only. Not relationships. And despite being too hip to live, according to her friends,

Margot was a throwback to a different time. A die-hard romantic, which was not exactly in sync with her New York lifestyle. She didn't want a tissue of a guy, to discard after one use. She wanted a keeper. But as time went by, and she got older and older—jeez, next March she'd be thirty—the reality of her life was getting harder to deny. She was lonely. Not for friends, she had those in spades. But for love. Or at least lust. The whole vibrator thing was getting old fast. She wanted someone to share her bed. And who knows, maybe Daniel Houghton III was the ticket.

She finished slicing the pizza and went inside. The gang glommed on to the food as if they hadn't eaten in weeks. All except Daniel, of course, who still looked as if he'd been transported through the looking glass. Poor baby. He had no idea what to make of his fellow tenants. His widened gaze moved over the group and ended up locking with hers. She smiled. He smiled back.

Oh, my. Heart flutters. Flutters lower down. All kinds of inexplicable flutters. She moved toward him, bearing appetizers. "Care for some?"

He hadn't looked away. Barely even blinked. Something was happening here. She wasn't sure if he was scared to death or interested. She chose to believe it was interest.

He finally glanced at the remainder of the pizza and took a small piece. She had time to admire his lovely teeth while he took a bite. Excellent hygiene. A plus in anyone's book. But God, she wanted to see him without that jacket. Actually, she wanted to see him in a lot less than that, but she'd settle.

She swung her platter-bearing hand to the right. "Take these, will ya?"

The platter was gone, and she had absolutely no interest in who'd taken over as hostess. Her focus was on Daniel. "It's just us," she said.

He blinked. She *loved* when he did that. Confusion on Daniel was like caviar on a blini. "Pardon?"

"Us. The gang. Informal."

This time he didn't blink. But his right eyebrow arched delightfully.

She decided to give him a tiny hint. Moving none too quickly—she didn't want him to spook—she maneuvered herself behind him, then reached over his broad shoulders and gently took hold of his lapels.

He jumped, and she thought she heard a little gasp. But he didn't stop her as she stripped him of the offending garment. She was so taken with what lay beneath, she let the jacket slip from her fingers.

Oh, he did work out. Yes indeedy. Those broad shoulders needed no help from padding. Her fingers itched to keep on going. To take off the purple tie, unbutton the oxford shirt. Touch the heat of his flesh. But since she didn't want him to run screaming to the police, she did the next best thing. She looked down at his butt.

Slim hips. Nice, nice, nice. And what an ass. She knew. She was something of a connoisseur when it came to that part of the anatomy, and if his wasn't worthy of a ten-minute standing ovation, then nothing was.

God, what an incredible hypocrite she was. She hated it when men were only interested in her body, either pro or con. Thought it was shallow and despicable. And here she was drooling over this virtual stranger. It was awful. Horrible. She'd have a serious talk with herself after she got in bed tonight. Eventually.

He turned, surprised to find his jacket puddled on the hardwood floor. "Is it dead?"

She grinned. "Not yet. Just wounded."

"I promise, next time I'll try harder to fit in."

"No. You're perfect."

He blushed. She couldn't believe how bad she was being. She was obviously channeling Samantha from *Sex and the City*. Cool.

After clearing his throat, he shook his head a little, and gave her a real hard look, squinching his eyes and everything. "I don't know how to talk to you."

"Most people don't."

"Does it get easier?"

She sighed. "Oh, yeah. Well, for the most part. I can be pretty strange."

"You sure make a mean pizza."

She grabbed his upper arms. Both of them. "Pizza."

"What?"

"Come with me."

He looked briefly to his left, to the door, then back at her. "Uh, now?"

"Yes, now." She let his shoulders go, but grabbed his hand, just in case he wanted to make a break for it. They walked past the big couch, the one she'd recovered in a dreamy cream suede, where Corrie, Anya and Rocco were laughing, past the hutch she'd gotten from her mother, into the kitchen.

The dough was on the counter. "You ever make a pizza?"

"I've ordered plenty."

She nodded. "Good enough." She handed him the rolling pin. "Roll it out."

He took to his task with the kind of concentration usually reserved for neurosurgeons. Eyebrows together, straight front teeth chewing on the lower lip. He attacked the round ball of dough, first pressing too hard, then easing up so much he didn't make a dent. But he learned quickly. Soon, he had the right pressure, he even had turned the dough and smoothed it out to a really even oval.

"You were kidding me, right?" she asked. "You studied pizza making for years."

He smiled and the effect it had on his face was nothing less then stellar. Holy Chihuahua! Before she could stop herself, she reached up and slipped his glasses off his face. His eyes widened with surprise. They were blue. Cerulean blue, which she'd seen on paint samples, but never on a living human. A person could swim in those eyes. Even his eyelashes made her swoon. Thick, dark, long.

"I need those," he said.

"Why?"

"To see."

"No. Why not contacts?"

"I tried them once. They were annoying."

"A little like me, huh?"

"You're not annoying."

"Ha." She got out the tomato sauce and the pepperoni. "Another, please," she said, nodding at the dough.

Daniel immediately went to work, this time very much at ease. "You're not. You're just different."

"From?"

"Other people I know."

"Ah."

He paused, took his glasses from where she'd left them on the counter and put them back on. "So you're a food stylist?"

"Yep."

"Which is what, exactly?"

"I make food look yummy. For magazines and television and at parties."

"I've heard they use mashed potatoes instead of ice cream on TV."

"Sometimes. Mashed potatoes don't melt under the lights."

He worked some more on the dough, this time making a perfect round. "How'd you get into food styling?"

She spread the sauce on the first pizza. "My parents owned a grocery store. Brooklyn's answer to Zabar's."

"Gourmet stuff?"

"Mostly cheeses and specialty items. But my mother used to like to give samples to the customers, and I liked to make the displays pretty."

"So it was a natural progression to doing the same thing professionally."

"Exactamundo."

He grinned. "Is there a lot of competition?"

"Lots. But I'm really, really good at it."

"I imagine you are."

Corrie walked into the kitchen. "Anya says her dinner is going to die an unnatural death if we don't go up to her place in five."

Margot frowned. "Okay. You guys go. Daniel and I will finish up the pizzas and bring them in ten."

Corrie nodded, but her gaze stayed on Daniel. "So what do you think?"

"About what?"

"Us. This. Margot."

"It's interesting. Not at all like Greenwich."

"That's a pretty big jump," Margot said as she spread pepperoni. "Why Chelsea?"

"I was ready for a change. Something big."

"Why?"

He shook his head. "You don't give up, do you?"

Margot stopped. Looked him right in the eyes. "Not until I get what I want."

Daniel's Adam's apple bobbed. "I see."

She smiled. She still didn't know why he'd moved to Chelsea, but she did know for certain why he'd moved to this building. To meet her, that's why. To become an adventure. A challenge. He might have been ready for something big, but she had the feeling he had no idea just how big the change was going to be.

"Well, I'll just see you two upstairs," Corrie said. She touched Daniel on the upper arm. "Don't be scared," she said, her voice gentle and calming. "She won't hurt you."

Daniel put down the rolling pin. "I'm not so sure."

Corrie laughed as she headed for the others.

Margot added the toppings to the first pizza, then stepped back. "Get creative, Daniel. Make this the best pizza you've ever had."

He looked at her in that way of his, as if he was trying to see underneath her mask to the alien life-form underneath. "Well, that wouldn't involve pineapple and ham."

She leaned against the counter to watch him. And as she suspected, he went traditional. Tomato sauce, oregano, garlic, sausage and mozzarella. With all the fresh, tasty surprises she'd spread out before him, he'd gone for the white bread. The mayo. As she saw it, she had a duty to step in. To introduce this man to the cornucopia of treats all around him. He lived in New York, for heaven's sake, the melting pot of the world, where one could get anything, anywhere, anytime. The hell with contact lenses, he needed to expand his frame of reference, to step out of the box he'd built around his life.

She had no idea about his architecture, but she'd be willing to bet her new job that it was as constricted and narrow as his pizza.

What she wasn't sure about was if he was willing to truly open his eyes, but so far, she had a good feeling about it. Hell, he'd put up with her weirdness, and she'd caused more than one man to leave skid marks on their mad dash out of her life.

He stepped back, eyed his creation. Then he reached for the basil.

Her heart swelled as he tore it into bits and sprinkled it over the cheese.

When he was finished, he turned to her, his eager smile proud, yet a little unsure.

She nodded. "Very, very nice."

"Fresh basil, huh?"

"One of nature's incredible wonders," she said, moving toward him. "And there's more."

His smile faltered the closer she got, but he stood his ground.

"There's rosemary and marjoram. Dill and lemongrass. All of them fragrant, some of them spicy. Meant to be tasted. Savored."

He swallowed again, and she couldn't blame him. She'd totally invaded his personal space. In fact, she was so near him she could smell the hint of his cologne, feel the heat of his breath on her cheek.

"You ready?" she asked.

"For what?" His voice was just above a whisper.

"Adventure. Excitement. Derring-do."

He blinked again. It was incredibly endearing and she wanted to lick his chin like a cat. "Sure."

"Okay then," she said. "Let's get those pizzas on the grill."

His mouth opened, but no words came out.

She sighed with happiness, then turned to the counter again. "Thank you," she whispered, to whoever was responsible.

He didn't move at all as she took the laden boards and left the kitchen. Hopefully, he'd join her. He wouldn't bolt, even though she'd left him the opportunity. She focused on her job, getting the food on the grill.

She didn't even look up when she heard the sliding-glass door open. She simply smiled.

4

DANIEL STOOD ON THE PATIO wondering what the hell he was doing there. Not the patio per se, but this situation, with Margot, grilling pizza. It was an experience that on the face of it shouldn't be bizarre, but it was. She was…

He didn't have a clue what or who she was. Different didn't say nearly enough. He'd never met anyone like her. Not even close.

The way she spoke. It was like being in a Quentin Tarantino film, sans the violence. He had absolutely no idea what would come out of her mouth next, and he couldn't remember the last time, if ever, that had happened to him. There was a rhythm to the conversations of his life, a logic. With her, there was nothing to hold on to.

"So, tell me more," she said.

"More about what?"

"You. Brothers, sisters, parents, friends. The entire scoop, please, leave nothing out."

He laughed. "It would put you to sleep, and you have to watch the grill."

"Try me."

He ran a hand through his hair, then moved to the far end of her patio to look over the edge. It would have been utterly appropriate if there had been an endless chasm below, but instead it was just the street with packed-in cars on both sides. "Well, my parents live in Port Washington."

"Ah, Long Island."

"Yep. I was raised there. I have an older sister, Gretchen."

"No brothers?"

"Nope."

"Me neither. Go on."

"My father's an architect."

"Do you work with him?"

"Nope. I didn't want to."

"Why not?"

Usually, if someone asked, he said he'd wanted to make it on his own. No one questioned that. It was an honest answer. But not a complete one. "I don't get along all that well with my father."

"Oh, bummer. Isn't he happy you followed in his footsteps?"

Daniel nodded. "Sure. And don't get me wrong, he's a good man. We just don't…" He shrugged.

"Talk?"

"Yeah."

"What about your mom?"

"She talks."

Margot smiled and it was like the sun moving from behind a cloud. She really was an extraordinary-looking woman. Lush, full, rounded. He kept wanting to touch her. Not that he would, but the urge was there. Her hair was incredibly shiny and thick, her skin glowed, and her eyes… When she looked at him it made his throat dry and his thoughts turn to mush. "Does she listen?"

"Who?"

Her soft laugh made the little hairs on the back of his neck stand up. In a good way. "Your mother."

"Sometimes. But mostly, she's concerned with her… With herself."

"I see." Margot looked at him for a long moment, then she turned back to the grill. "These are done. Let's take 'em to Anya's."

He got the boards, and she put the pizzas, which smelled incredible, on them. Then she led him through the apartment to the front door. He glanced at his jacket, still crumpled on the floor. There would be time for that later.

HE CHECKED HIS WATCH and frowned at the time. It was almost one in the morning. He had to be up at six for work. At least they'd reached the end of the extended dinner. They were at Rocco's, whose place was just as unexpected as everything else had been over the long night.

The ex-boxer collected antiques. And he had one hell of an eye. They were seated in his living room, on elegant Louis XIV chaises. Across from Daniel on the smaller couch, Eric rested his head on Devon's lap. Corrie sat cross-legged on the Persian rug with her back upright, as if she were standing at attention. It would have been impossible for him, but evidently her training as a dancer had been primarily about posture.

Anya was in the kitchen with Rocco making tea. And Margot… Margot sat inches away from Daniel, her back against a silk pillow, her legs up on the chaise, her bare feet nearly touching his thigh. She'd painted her nails a brilliant scarlet, and she had rings, one white, one blue, around two of her toes.

He kept his hands cupped around his brandy snifter but all he could think about was running his fingers down the enticing curve of her foot.

It was nuts. He wasn't into feet. He knew some men were, but he'd never given them a thought.

He stole a look at Margot and was shocked to meet her very intense gaze. He wanted to look away, but he couldn't.

"It's all right, you know," she said, her voice very soft, meant only for him.

"What's all right?" he whispered back.

"You can touch them."

His mouth opened, but, again, nothing. No response. Not a clue what to say.

"They're pretty rings," she went on. "I got one of them at a flea market. The blue one was a gift."

His gaze finally moved from hers only to stare at the exotic toe jewelry. An image flashed in his mind, very vivid. So vivid, he had to shift on the couch.

"What?" she asked, leaning a little forward.

"Nothing."

"Come on, Daniel. We know each other too well to hold back now."

He looked at her again. At the teasing smile, the coy arch of her eyebrow. "I don't know you at all."

"I'm an open book. Ask me anything."

He raised the snifter to his lips and took a big sip. The heat slithered down his throat, expanding as it reached his chest. "Do you have rings anywhere else?" he asked.

She nodded.

He coughed. Turned away. Stared at an eighteenth-century highboy.

"Do you want to know where?"

Her voice snuck beneath his defenses, which weren't many. He was too full, too drunk and too bewildered by the woman. He'd talked to the others tonight, but cursorily. Even when he wanted to, he couldn't force his attention far away from Margot. Willing himself to be cool, to not let her know what she was doing to him, he sipped again at the brandy. But it was no use. He wanted to know about her other rings. Badly. He sighed. Then nodded.

Again, that soft, knowing chuckle. "Well, I have these," she said.

He looked. He was constitutionally incapable of not looking. But all he saw were her hands. Long, beautiful hands with crimson nails. She did have rings. On each hand. One a pearl, the other a diamond. His chest sank with disappointment, which he realized was nuts. It's just that she was so…exotic, he was expecting more. Different. Erotic.

Then she leaned forward even more. When she had his gaze locked, she licked her lower lip with the tip of her pink tongue. "The others will have to wait until we're alone."

"Others?"

She smiled, showing him her white teeth. "Two more. But I'm not going to tell you where. You'll have to see for yourself."

"Oh, God."

Laughing, she leaned back against her pillow.

The next thing he knew, she'd swung her legs off the

chaise and stood. "Well, kiddies. It's late, and I have a disgustingly early call. Thank you all for a magnificent evening. I look forward to next Sunday's soiree where I shall be making dessert." She pointed to Corrie. "You're appetizers." Her red-tipped finger moved to Devon and Eric. "Main course." Then she pointed at Daniel. "You'll help me."

She walked toward the kitchen. "I'm leaving," she said to Anya and Rocco, who were just coming back to the living room. "I have to go. Thank you for everything." She kissed both of them on the cheek. "Take care of each other." Then she was at the front door. She waved her fingers. Closed the door behind her.

For the first time since he'd met her, Daniel got a full breath. He sagged against the chaise, still boggled by the night.

Corrie approached him. She patted his knee. "See? I told you it would be okay. I think it's wonderful."

"What?"

"You and Margot, of course."

"What are you talking about?"

Across the way, Devon chuckled. "You'll see."

Daniel looked at the man. "See what? What's going on?"

Eric yawned expansively, then sat up. "Nothing to worry about, Daniel old boy. Just relax. She'll be gentle."

Daniel stood up. Put the snifter on the table. "I don't know what the hell you people are talking about. If it's some kind of cult—"

Laughter cut him off. He didn't realize he'd said anything funny.

"It's not a cult," Corrie said. "It's just Margot. And she's wonderful. Kind and caring. She just wants to help."

"With what? I don't need any help."

Corrie's gaze raked him from head to toe then back again. She smiled kindly, with just a hint of pity. "You're so sweet," she said.

"This is insane," he said, bewildered by this wacko group he'd stumbled into. "All of you."

"Yep, but we mean no harm. So don't fret."

"Thanks for the advice," he said, heading to the door. "And I don't think I'll be available next Sunday. I've got a previous engagement."

No one tried to change his mind, but they gave each other disturbingly knowing looks. He had to get out of there. Now. This was out of control. And he wanted no part of it.

MARGOT HAD TO GET TO SLEEP. Tomorrow, actually today, was really important, and she couldn't screw it up. But she couldn't stop thinking about Daniel.

She'd been bad. Naughty, naughty. But it had been so much fun teasing him. He blushed! It was completely adorable, and she couldn't wait to make him do it again. And again.

She shifted under her comforter, punched her pillow into submission, but thoughts of Daniel just kept on coming. Halfway through dinner, she realized that teasing Daniel was way up there on her hit parade. Kind of like chocolate. Addictive, satisfying, good for the libido. She kept wanting more and more, until that silly little stunt on the couch. Could she have been more blatant?

Jeez, it was amazing she'd held herself back from ravishing the boy right there in front of God and everybody.

She just hoped she hadn't scared him into moving back to Greenwich.

Nah. He'd liked it. She remembered his eyes, how they'd gleamed with interest. How they'd come back to her over and over again, no matter what else was going on in the room. That was truly something.

She knew she had an effect on men. Mostly, they were just confused by her, but from time to time she elicited real interest. Which pleased her so much that she'd always, always, make a judicious exit, before the thrill had a chance to dissipate. Always leave them wanting more was her motto. And yet with Daniel, she wasn't so anxious to run off. Not that she could. She lived here. But it wouldn't be that difficult to make herself scarce.

No. She didn't want to do that. She wanted to experience the rush of last night all over again. It was exhilarating. Thrilling. Exciting in a way that hadn't happened to her since… Since ever.

"Wow," she whispered to the night. "Wow, wow." Then she turned over again. She really needed to get to sleep. Now.

Reaching down to her bedside drawer, she pulled out her favorite toy. She had lots of yummy things to imagine tonight. Too many. How could she possibly choose just one?

But one did come to mind the moment she touched herself with her vibrator. Daniel. Naked. Investigating her rings. All of them.

HE WAS A MORON. No doubt about it. Daniel wiped his face with his hand, cringing at the vision he saw in the mirror. He looked like hell, and today was not the day for it. He'd known about the presentation. Had worked for months getting his plans together, making sure he'd included everything the clients could possibly want, and what did he do the night before?

"Idiot," he said to the man in the mirror. "Moron."

Then he pushed his hair back with his fingers, straightened his shoulders and strode out of the bathroom. His boss, Edgar Kogen, was waiting impatiently by Daniel's desk. "They're here."

Daniel nodded, wishing he'd had time for another cup of coffee before he had to do the dog-and-pony show. But he got his portfolio and followed Kogen into the conference room.

He had already prepared the room. There were easels covered with detail drawings which, along with what he had in his portfolio, would convince the attorneys from Bressler, Wendelken and Sherman that this new building would handle all their needs for years to come. He pasted a smile on his face, and launched into his spiel.

It took five hours, but by the end of it, the attorneys were sold. They shook hands, and Daniel caught Edgar's approving nod as he gathered his drawings. This was a major, prestige deal, one worth millions. Daniel had been privy to the competition's approach, seen sketches, which were damn good. But they were too modern, too forward thinking for the stodgy attorneys. Bressler et al were from the old school, like the company Daniel worked for. Like his father. They liked the status quo, and that's just what Daniel had given them. So what if it wasn't exciting, so what if he'd had to force himself to think like an old man when he'd drawn up the designs.

These men in their wool suits would be shocked if they knew what Daniel did in his spare time. That he created fantasies; futuristic buildings. His passion, one he kept close to the vest, was science fiction. He'd discovered Frank Frazetta years ago when he'd started hiding paperback fantasy books under his bed. Then it was H. R. Giger and hundreds of other visionary artists who blew away all the old concepts about what things could be. Whenever he was upset or bored he would take to his drawings, letting his imagination run wild. But that was all behind closed doors. What he did in the real world was design buildings that looked like other buildings. Old buildings.

He was alone in the conference room. His portfolio was zipped, the table littered with unused notepads, empty coffee cups, carafes half-full of ice water. He wondered why he didn't feel more elated. It was a big deal, what he'd done. A raise wouldn't be out of the question. His partnership was coming into focus. And yet, he couldn't muster so much as a satisfied grin.

Tired, that's all. He hadn't slept well. Hardly at all. Tonight, after the gym, he'd crash early. By tomorrow he'd be himself again.

He went out, toward his office. The receptionist, Jill, smiled broadly and gave him two thumbs up. He answered her with a nod and felt guilty that it wasn't more. She was a nice woman, and she was always there to assist whenever he needed her. But his mind was already back at the Chelsea apartment. Not on a good night's sleep though. His jacket. He'd left it at Margot's. He should get it after work. Simple, really. No big deal. She'd be tired, too. He wouldn't stick around.

He wouldn't even think about those other two rings or where they were hidden on that incredible body.

To: The Gang at Eve's Apple
From: Margot
Sub: HOLY MOLY!
Dear Everybody,
I'm at work. Chaos reins and hellhounds abound, but I don't care. I have to write this because I can't stop thinking about it. Him. Daniel.

I mentioned we had a new guy move in to the building, right? Well, he came to the weekly dinner last night, and OMG!!! He's GORGEOUS. Seriously. Heart stoppingly. I mean it. He's beyond the beyond. Okay, so he's clueless about what to wear or how to wear it, but the potential is there. I feel like Michelangelo when he saw the marble that would become David. All I have to do is strip away the parts that aren't truly Daniel.

But even more important than his makeover possibilities, I liked him. Yeah, that way. There was this…thing between us. Sparks. Magic. Heat. I kept wanting to lick him all over. It was overwhelming. He talks. He has a sense of humor. He's artistic. Well, he's an architect, so I'm assuming there, but I think so. And he wanted…more. Me, I supposed. Which is…

Anyway. I'm hereby throwing my hat in the ring. (Maybe we should change that to throwing our panties into the ring.) Daniel is officially my Man To Do. I wish it could be more, but I have serious doubts.

He's not Jewish. Which, as you know, isn't a requirement, but Daniel is *so* not. He's so conservative. But curious. I just hope he's not overwhelmed by it all. I mean, I live in ethnic-alternate-lifestyle land. He comes from a world of white bread and mayo. I have the feeling his parents would expire on the spot if he should bring me to meet them. But, I digress. He's a man to do. I'm just hoping he's a man to do a LOT.

I need to get back to work. I'm doing onion rings, and I smell like I've been deep-fried. I'll keep you posted.

Love and smooches,

Margot

5

DANIEL THREW HIS JACKET on the back of the couch and walked straight to the kitchen. It was almost eight, and he'd thought he'd never get out of the office. Edgar had wanted to talk about the new building. And talk. All Daniel had wanted to do was go home.

Tired, that's all. He pulled a beer out of the fridge, popped the top, but stopped short of drinking. He would just go up and get the jacket he'd left at Margot's. No big deal. She was probably just as tired as he was, and like him, she would want to make it an early, easy night. He wouldn't bother her. Except to get the jacket, of course. Just that.

He put the beer down on the counter and went toward the door. She might not even be home. She had that TV commercial and all, which probably kept her busy until late.

The whole way up the stairs he debated turning around. Until he actually knocked, he wasn't completely sure he would. But then the door opened, and there was Margot, and she broke into a smile that made him feel like the king of the world.

"You're just on time," she said, stepping back so he could walk inside.

"For what?"

"Dinner."

"Oh, no." He watched as she shut the door, his gaze meandering down the silky orange tunic that covered her curves. It was tighter across her breasts, just enough for him to get a teasing image of their shape. "My jacket."

"Is right over there," she said, pointing to an ottoman at the far end of the room.

Things had changed since last night. There were big pillows on the floor next to the low teak coffee table. There was a big ceramic pitcher on the table with a raised picture of an Egyptian cat. There were two plates, two bowls, two napkins, both in gold rings, two wineglasses. "You're expecting someone."

Margot came to his side. "Sit down. It's almost ready."

He turned to face her.

She smiled serenely, nodding twice. "On the pillow," she said. Then she pointed to the cushion closest to the couch.

He didn't understand, which, it seemed, was par for the course with Margot. He sat, awkwardly, trying to fold his legs underneath the table, his shoes getting in the way.

By the time he was settled, Margot had disappeared into the kitchen. He looked again at the table. She'd set it for two, but she couldn't have known he was coming over. Could she?

She came back, her skirt flowing, her long hair pulled back into a loose ponytail that hung down her back.

There was a flower, the same orange as her dress, behind her right ear. Her lips looked smooth and creamy, although he wasn't sure if she had lipstick on, or if they were dewy from her tongue's ministrations. His throat felt dry and he was glad to see the wine bottle in her hand.

She showed him the label, but he didn't even glance at it. He didn't look at his glass when she poured, either. He just kept staring at her mouth.

Her smile brought him back from wherever he'd been, and he gave himself a mental shake. "I'm…"

"What?" she asked, moving to the other side of the table. She picked up the pitcher, brought it to her face and took a long, closed-eyes breath. Then she leaned across the table. "Put your hands over the bowl," she said in a smoky whisper that went straight to his groin.

He obeyed mindlessly, his gaze captured not by her mouth but by the sight of her breasts. The tops, to be precise, revealed as the silk of her dress fell open and he was allowed a forbidden glimpse. They were perfect, pale, rounded. His hands, held over the wooden bowls, ached to cross the distance between them.

He jumped when he felt the water. She was pouring water over his fingers. It was warm, and it smelled like flowers.

Her soft chuckle brought his gaze to meet hers. What he saw there was more than amusement. There was an invitation in her eyes that had nothing to do with dinner.

Which was good, because he doubted he could eat.

She put the pitcher on the table, leaned over with her hand on his shoulder, and whispered, "I'll be right back."

What the hell was happening to him? This was nuts.

Completely. He got near Margot and his brain turned to mush. The lower part of his body had the opposite problem. Jeez, he was hard. Sitting on this incredibly uncomfortable pillow, with his left foot falling asleep, something poking into the small of his back, he was unmistakably erect. Thank goodness he was hidden under the table, because his pants weren't up to the task of disguising the issue.

And he could probably take his hands away from the bowl now.

Okay, he was blushing. He felt the blood in his cheeks, and it made him almost as uncomfortable as the stupidity of his dick. He sighed as he pulled the napkin from the ring and dried off.

He should have stuck with the plan. Gotten his jacket and left. But she'd done something to him, spiked the air, hypnotized him.

He'd never reacted this way before. Not that he hadn't been attracted to women, but no one had ever turned him into a blabbering idiot like this. He couldn't speak, he couldn't stop staring at her, he clearly couldn't control his body. It was…

"This is bstilla," she said.

He jumped again, completely surprised that she was standing at his side. "What?

"Bstilla," she repeated, putting a plate down on the table. "And these are lamb kabobs."

He looked at the second platter. That one he sort of recognized, although he'd always seen kabobs on skewers. These were bits of lamb on small beds of green. But the first dish was a mystery. It looked like very thinly rolled pastry with some kind of filling. All bite-size.

"It's a traditional Moroccan first course," she said as she gracefully lowered herself to the cushion across from him, "although I'm serving them as an *amuse bouche*."

"Amuse…?"

"Little bites that delight the mouth. After this, we'll have tajine, batinjaan, couscous and khubz. For dessert, there's fruit and pastry with mint tea. We eat everything with our fingers." She demonstrated by taking one of the bstilla between her finger and thumb and popping it in her mouth. Her eyes closed as she chewed. Her low moan made him think of something completely inappropriate. Finally, she looked at him again. "Go on."

He took one, still hot from the oven. He ate it whole and his mouth filled with spice and chicken. He swallowed hard as his eyes filled with tears. He made a sound, hoping she wouldn't be insulted when he died.

In an instant, she was on her feet. She disappeared while he was trying to wave the flames shooting out of his mouth. But then she was back, handing him a glass of milk.

He drank, the cool liquid putting out the fire like magic. "Thank you."

"Little too spicy there, Daniel?"

"A bit."

"I tend to go a little nuts. I have a really high tolerance for heat. I'm sorry. I should have warned you."

"It was good," he said, his voice only cracking a little.

Her right eyebrow rose.

"No, really. There was some definite flavor in there. Right before the incredible pain."

When she laughed, her face became a work of art. She was beautiful anyway, but the laughter made everything shine. He couldn't resist joining her, and then when calmed, she sipped some wine, and he did that with her, too.

"Nothing else is that spicy," she said. "The tajine isn't bland, but it's not too bad. Try a little first."

He nodded and reached for the kebab. The meat smelled great. He took a tentative bite, but this was pure pleasure, no agony at all. He realized how hungry he was as he lifted another morsel from the plate.

She ate another b-thingy and seemed to enjoy it tremendously. Her gaze was on his, never wavering, and it was weird, because it wasn't awkward at all. He watched her, she watched him, and they enjoyed the food and the scents and the push and pull that wafted over the table. His fingers got messy, but it felt right, and then when he dipped them in the water, he wondered why there weren't finger bowls with every meal.

"How did it go?" she asked him.

He didn't want to ask her what she meant. For once, he wanted to figure out her non sequitur, and not look like a dunce. Ah, he'd told her about today's presentation. "I got it."

"That's wonderful. Then this is a celebration dinner. How cool."

"Thanks," he said. "How did you know I'd be here?"

"You left your jacket."

"But I could have come anytime. I could have called. The meal is ready."

She got that enigmatic grin that stirred him in low

places. "You haven't had much mystery in your life, have you?"

"Mystery? No."

"Well, you do now."

"That's it? That's all you're going to say?"

"Yep. Have another kabob."

He did. They were fantastic. Crunchy on the outside, tender as butter on the inside. "What about you?"

"Oh, I have lots of mystery in my life. I'm confounded daily."

"By what?"

"Everything. Everybody. There was a guy on the subway this morning who burst out laughing when a kid slipped and fell. I mean, why would someone think that was funny. The kid was hurt and embarrassed, and all alone. And this guy with a scraggly beard is laughing at him like it's the highlight of his week."

"But that happens all the time. People laugh at others' misfortunes because it's not them in the hot seat. It's relief."

"I've thought about that, but underneath that is a meanness I don't get. A human meanness. That it's inherent to our humor is the puzzle."

"It's never happened to you?"

She nodded. "Yeah, it has. Which really bugs me. I'm not as bad as the scraggly beard, but I've had my moments."

"I can't imagine you being intentionally mean."

"I try not to be, but I'm just like everyone else."

"Oh, no. You're not. Not even close."

She put her fingers in the bowl and wiggled them

around. "Now, Daniel, am I supposed to take that as a compliment?"

"Yes."

"Goody." She stood up, came to his side. After taking his plate, she crouched down so her gaze was even with his. "I've been wanting to do this," she said. Then she leaned over and put her lips on his.

It was a kiss like the woman. Unique, surprising. He wanted to press harder, to taste her, but he waited, curious about what she would do.

For a long moment it was simply touching. Soft, closed lips. Her scent, not lavender, but something flowery. The realization of her proximity, that he could touch her if he just moved his hand a few inches. Behind his closed eyes he saw her laughing, saw the alluring curve of her breast.

Then her lips parted, just enough. Always a quick study, he opened, too, and her breath slipped inside him. Again, she took her time, taking his breath and returning it warmer.

When he finally felt the tip of her tongue on his lower lip, he shivered. It almost woke up his sleeping foot.

She sighed as she teased him, touching tentatively, learning the texture of his lips, the shape of his teeth.

He couldn't do this anymore. The stillness was more than he was capable of. He touched her tongue with his. Tasted her wet heat. Moaned at the spices that ignited him in a whole different way.

Then she was gone. Leaving his mouth agape, his breath hovering somewhere outside his body. When he opened his eyes, he saw her thighs. Covered by the thin material, he could still make out their shape, and he could imagine the softness of her skin there.

She walked away, as he knew she would, leaving him with his problem rearing its head again, so to speak. "Damn."

He shook his head and tried to make sense of what had just happened. She'd kissed him, which shouldn't have been a major deal, but it was. Very major. Sanity-threatening major. He knew he was going to make love to her, and that it would be an experience unlike any other. He didn't know if it would happen tonight, next week, or next year, but it would happen. It was no longer a choice. It was an imperative, like breathing or sleeping. And frankly, it scared the hell out of him.

MARGOT GOT TO THE KITCHEN and when she knew he couldn't see her even if he turned around, she slumped against the counter. She'd kissed him. He'd kissed her back. And he'd blown her socks off.

What shocked her almost as much was the way she was with him. Good lord, she was a femme fatale, a siren, a vamp. And sexy? *She'd* go to bed with herself, she was so damn seductive.

Her heart still raced, her legs wobbled and she could hardly see straight. From a guy she barely knew, who had the style of a stalk of broccoli, who blushed at the drop of a double entendre.

But the truth of it was, despite this moment of reflection and disbelief, when she was in that room with him, she felt like a goddess. Oz, the great and powerful. It was unbelievable, unprecedented. And so, so fantastic.

She gathered herself together and plated the rest of the food. Couscous on a large platter, the flat bread in a tea towel, salads in small bowls, and then the chicken tajine in her aunt Sadie's soup crock.

She took the platter and the salads first, putting them in the center of the table. Daniel watched her avidly, as if every second held a surprise. It made her aware of her arms, the way she moved, especially as she bent in front of him.

His gaze went right to her ass, and for the first time in like forever she didn't mind. She was always self-conscious about her butt, and she should be panicky with Daniel staring wide-eyed and tongue-tied. Instead, she felt as if she had the best behind in all the boroughs. Go figure.

"It smells great."

She laughed even though she knew he was talking about the food. "Thanks. Almost done." She walked away, shakin' it a whole lot more than she would, say, at the butcher's.

The last of the dinner looked perfect and she took it to the table, bending this time so he could check out her breasts again. It was incredible, the way he looked at her. As if he could barely contain himself from ravishing her right on the couscous platter.

She moved her pillow closer to him, touching distance, then sat down. He stared at her again, swallowing, hardly blinking. She wanted to take his glasses off, ruffle his hair, loosen his tie. But that was for after dinner.

If only she didn't have to be up at the crack of dawn tomorrow. Tonight, she'd have to be careful. Take him only so far. Which was probably good. She knew from being an avid watcher of far too much television that the minute the sexual tension was satisfied, all kinds of things could go wrong. Interest could peter out like a deflated balloon. Teasing was the ticket. Making him crazy. It was clear she had a talent for it. Maybe she should give up the whole food styling thing and become a professional vamp.

She brushed the side of his hand with her knuckles. He tried, poor baby, not to react, but react he did. It was glorious. More delicious than the tajine. "In Morocco," she said, "some people eat couscous with a spoon, but I prefer balls."

He blinked. "Pardon me?"

"Watch," she said, fighting a grin. She used her thumb and two fingers to roll a small ball of the grain, which was just sticky enough to accomplish the task. Once it was formed, she held it up to Daniel's mouth. "Open."

He obeyed. Just like that. She should have shot it in there, but instead she placed it on his tongue, making sure he was aware that her fingers were right there, too.

Then she felt his tentative tongue. Fast, as if he hoped she wouldn't notice. She bit on the sides of her lip so she wouldn't smile.

He chewed slowly. Swallowed.

"Now you," she said, so softly the words were like a sigh.

He rolled the couscous as he'd showed her. Brought it haltingly to her lips. She opened her mouth and he mimicked her again, putting the morsel on her tongue. She closed her lips around his fingers, trapping them.

At first, his eyes widened, but as she licked him slowly his lids grew heavy and his breathing became shallow. She understood completely.

She let him go, putting his hand on the table, wanting to say something clever, but all she managed was, "Oh, my."

He blinked his response. Looked at the table. "You're unbelievable." Then his gaze came up again.

She felt the pounding of her heart and the pulse between her legs as she looked into his eyes. "Believe."

6

DANIEL ATE, although he wasn't the least bit hungry. Not for the food. His whole body had been jolted, not just the obvious parts. His skin felt hypersensitive, every scent curled inside him in swirls that fought for attention. And his fingers, where she'd licked him, tingled as if they'd been awakened from a long sleep.

Margot ate, too, but her gaze stayed firmly on him. Mischief sparked her dark eyes, a smile played at the corners of her lush lips. He should do something. Move closer to her, touch her. God knows he wanted to. Wanted everything promised behind those long lashes.

Who was he kidding? He was completely out of his depth. This woman enticed him, but she also bewildered him. It was as if he was in a movie, and he hadn't read the script. He ate some of the salad, which was just as exotic as everything else she'd served him. Like the woman.

He'd grown up in a family where every Monday was meat loaf, Tuesdays were turkey breast, etc., etc. The most unusual thing his mother served was wagon-wheel pasta.

He hadn't had Thai until college. This Moroccan meal was a first. The tajine had turned out to be a stew, but nothing like the dried, rubbery beef of his childhood.

It wasn't as if he was a complete naïf. He'd been to

some of the best restaurants in New York, seen shows, strolled Times Square after midnight. He'd had his share of women, too, but good God.

His last girlfriend, Emily, had been a Dartmouth Ph.D. candidate studying pre-Colombian art. He tried to picture her sucking his fingers during dinner, but the image wouldn't form. Actually, he couldn't picture her sucking his fingers anytime. She was a pale blonde with delicate wrists and a passion for obscure poetry. He'd liked her, even though the sex, while it had been infrequent, had been pretty awful.

And here he was, Barney Fife, dining with a cross between Angelina Jolie and Jessica Rabbit.

"What's that smile about?"

"Nothing. Everything."

"Come on, Daniel. You know you can't keep secrets from me."

"I can't?"

She shook her head. "I have my ways."

"I don't doubt it."

"So?"

He leaned back on the couch. He'd given up all hope of having feelings in his lower legs. "I was thinking about my ex-girlfriend."

Margot's eyebrow arched dramatically. "I think I'm offended."

"No, I'm not thinking about her that way. Emily was, uh, nice."

"Nice."

"A doctoral candidate at Dartmouth."

"Ah."

"She liked Wagner. A lot."

"'Ride of the Valkyries'?"

He nodded.

"Did she take you to Valhalla?"

He laughed. "Not so I noticed."

"Oh, too bad."

"Hence the emphasis on the ex."

"I see. And how long ago was this?"

"About eight months."

She popped a couscous ball. Licked her lower lip.

"What about you?" he asked as he studied that lip.

"I have no ex-girlfriends."

"Cute."

"My last boyfriend was not a good fellow."

Daniel paused halfway to his finger bowl. "He hurt you?"

"No, not physically. He did some damage to the heart, however."

"I'm sorry."

She shook her head, making her ponytail flip to her shoulder. "Heartaches are part of the growing process, no? I learned."

"Learned what?"

"That sometimes what looks dangerous really is dangerous. That I can put up with almost anything but lies."

"Ah."

She stood, and his gaze moved down her body. It wasn't something he was able to control. He had to look.

"I'll get dessert."

He watched her until he'd stretched his neck as far as possible. Then he finished washing his fingers, the water cooler now. He must remember not to lie to Margot. That wouldn't be difficult. He wasn't much for lies himself. But the whole danger thing? Daniel thought of leather, motorcycles, dark alleys. Which were about as far away from him as the moon.

What was he doing here? Was he a game to her? He pushed the table back so he could stretch his legs, wincing at the pins and needles.

She came back bearing a tray of fruit and baklava. She put it down in front of him, and he didn't stop to think. He just took her by the arm and pulled her down to his lap.

She gasped, fell back into his arms, looked at him with wide eyes and her mouth a perfect O.

With adrenaline taking over, he leaned forward. Right into a kiss. The moment his lips touched hers, it was all over for higher mental functions. He was lost in soft heat. Her mouth was slightly open and her warm breath mingled with his. Although he wanted to look at her, he kept his eyes closed, the better to focus on her taste, her scent.

The tip of her tongue slipped between his teeth, bringing with it a new peak of arousal. He was hard, pushing against his trousers. But her tongue chased those thoughts away, bringing him right back to the incredible things she was doing to him above the waist.

He explored her, feeling an amazing sense of freedom to linger, to tease, to let go. When he thrust inside as he never dared to do with Em, Margot arched in his arms, moaned so that he felt the vibration in his lips. This was more like his fantasies than anything that had ever happened to him in real life. He was such a damn nice guy. Never crossed the line, never took more than his share. Never behaved like the man he was in the dark of night, when he was alone with his hand and his fantasies.

Margot gave him permission, with her flashing eyes and her wicked grin.

Her hand went to the back of his neck. She stroked him there with gentle fingers, barely touching him, just stirring the small hairs. He shivered and caught her lower lip between his teeth.

Her sharp gasp told him he hadn't gone too far. Perhaps he hadn't gone far enough. But just as he moved, so he could plunge into her mouth again, her hand left his neck, and then she sat up. So much for his instincts.

"Why, Daniel," she said, her soft voice tinged with breathlessness. "I'm…"

"Oh, shit. I'm sorry."

"Sorry?" She braced her hand on the coffee table, then stood.

When he looked up at her, he wasn't surprised at the flush on her cheeks. Or the way she couldn't look straight at him.

"Why are you sorry? That was… Wow."

"Wow?"

"I thought so."

"Then why…?"

She smiled. "I have to get up at five."

"Oh."

She sighed. "That isn't the only reason."

He knew it. At least his erection had withered, which

normally wasn't a good thing, but in this case, he was grateful.

Margot crouched beside him. "I'd like to do this slowly," she said, lightly stroking his arm. "I'd like to do this right."

"It's too soon."

She nodded.

"Well, sure. We just met." He stood, taking her hand as he rose so they faced each other. So they were close. "I'd better…"

"Yeah."

"But maybe we can—"

"I'd like that."

"This weekend?"

Her smile gave him back his courage. "Thanks for dinner. It was really great."

"You're welcome. And congratulations."

It took him a minute to remember the office. "Ah, thanks." He thought about kissing her again, but rejected the idea. Instead, he walked toward the door. As he was leaving, he looked at her once more. Her hair was messed up, the flower gone. Her lipstick had smeared just a bit on the right corner. It hurt him how he wanted her.

She blew him a kiss as the door closed.

MARGOT FELL ON THE COUCH, grateful she was close, because she would have crumpled to the floor. She couldn't believe what had happened. Couldn't believe the way he'd kissed her. Couldn't believe she'd sent him home. It had been a lot easier standing in the kitchen, deciding she needed to slow down than when they were actually face-to-face. One more minute and she would have caved.

"Oh, God, am I in trouble," she whispered. The thing to do here was to put the dishes in the kitchen and get her butt to bed. But she couldn't move. Every bone in her body had turned to jelly.

She'd never, not in her whole life, been the woman she'd been with Daniel. Confident. Sensual. Dominant. There was just something about him, with his gorgeous full lips and those wide, innocent eyes, that made her go supervixen.

But then, he'd kissed her, and somewhere in that tentative, trying-too-hard-not-to-hurt-her touch, she'd felt something else. Something strong. Fire.

She wanted more. To find Daniel's inner beast and let him loose. He needed it. She needed it. Bad.

She got it together to lean forward far enough to grab his drink from the table. After slaking her thirst, she put the glass down and flopped back on the cushions. The dishes would have to wait. It was necessary to get to her bed, take off her clothes, fall asleep. But that would have to wait, too.

Her eyes closed as she remembered the feel of his hand on her wrist, pulling her down to his lap. Très Conan. Incredibly yummy. Oh, God. Had she ever been this horny before?

Nope.

So why in hell wasn't she ravishing the man right this second?

Because, it seemed painfully clear, she was insane. Out of her mind. Scared.

She forced herself to her feet. Grabbed two platters and went to the kitchen. For the next twenty minutes, all she did was wash dishes, put away food, beat herself up for being such a coward.

Which didn't make sense. She'd been an Amazon with him. Me Jane, you Tarzan. But when it came down to the real stuff, beyond the games and the teasing, she'd chickened out like the worm she truly was.

Therapy. That's what she needed. By a whole team of psychiatrists.

Maybe it had something to do with Gordon. She'd talked about him so casually to Daniel. "I learned," she said, mocking her own lying bull. She'd learned, all right, but not the lessons she'd implied. Gordon had taught her that she was an idiot when it came to men. That she was so easy to manipulate, she made puppets looks macho. He'd won her over with pretty words, walked into her world and turned it upside down. Not in a good way.

She'd been her usual oblivious self, "helping" him to find his own style, taking him to the best shops. He'd dressed for her, he'd cut his hair for her, he'd gotten new shoes.

Then he'd lied. He'd stolen. He'd made her think he was someone he wasn't, and even when the evidence was there, right in front of her nose, she'd refused to see it.

And it had taken her so, so long to stop wanting him, which was maybe the worst thing of all. How could she want someone like Gordon? How could she have ached for him, thought she would die if she couldn't have him?

And how could she trust herself again?

Of course, Daniel was the anti-Gordon. At least, he appeared to be. Sweet, gentle, innocent. Kind to a fault. But hadn't Gordon seemed like a sweetie pie when she'd first met him?

Part of her couldn't believe that Daniel was hiding a dark side. On the other hand, there'd been that moment. That stunning power that had taken her utterly by surprise when he'd…

And that had been the moment she'd had to say stop. When she knew she couldn't trust herself one tiny bit. Because the moment he got all butch and bad, all her buttons had been pushed. She'd wanted him, wanted that, wanted his bad boy to come out and ravish her until she couldn't move.

Which wasn't a good thing.

The perfection of Daniel was that he was a nice guy. On the surface…

7

"Margot, sweetheart, just this one time. Please. For your mother, who loves you."

Margot pulled the phone away from her ear and made a face. Which was juvenile, but then she was talking to her mother. She brought the phone back. "Fine. I'll go, but I don't even like Estelle."

"It's going to be a lovely wedding. Everyone will be there, you won't even have to talk to her."

"I don't want to buy her a wedding present. She regifted the last one. Back to me!"

"We both know she has no taste. Look at the guy she's marrying. *Oy!*"

Margot poured herself a cup of coffee, then took it to the living room. "How are Dad's dishes?"

"Don't get me started on the dishes. That man is going to drive me to an early grave. Like he'd know bone china from *red* China. I tell you, it takes the patience of a saint."

"Ma, he enjoys it. What does it hurt?"

"What does it hurt? Have you seen the hole in my front-door screen? Of course you have, it's been there six months. And did I mention the crack on the wall in the bathroom? The whole house is going to cave in and he won't notice because he's buying *shmates* on eBay."

Margot sipped, glad the subject was no longer her cousin Estelle, the most annoying woman in Queens. The knock on her door made her smile. An excuse, which was just what she needed. "Ma, I have to go. I have company, and then I have to go to work."

"Call me later."

"I will." She hung up and went to the door. It was the boys. "Well?"

They came in, Devon flopping on the couch while Eric went right for the kitchen.

"He wasn't happy," Eric said over his shoulder.

"He will be when it's over," Margot said, hoping she was right and the guys hadn't scared Daniel back to Greenwich. "You know where you're going?"

"Ricky's," Devon said.

"Then, if he's still with us, Abercrombie & Fitch," Eric added.

Margot nodded, then looked at her watch. She had to be at work at ten, and that didn't leave much time. Normally, she wouldn't have to work on a Saturday, but the shoot was way behind schedule, which, according to the director, was all her fault. She turned back to Devon. "Some retro, some Euro. And the jeans—"

"We know," Eric said, interrupting from the other room.

"I just want to make sure," she said, as she returned to the kitchen where she'd left her pocketbook. "We can't scare him."

"Too late."

"Ha." She checked to make sure she had money for a cab. She was too late to do the subway thing. "Where's Corrie?"

Devon frowned. "Nels didn't come home last night."

"Oh, no."

Eric came back from the kitchen with two mugs of coffee. "You're going to have to see to her until we get back."

"I will. God, I hate that man."

"She doesn't," Devon said. "I wish she would."

"Doesn't he know what he's got in Corrie? She's too damn good for him."

"Amen," Eric said, shoving his lover's legs to the side so he could sit. "She's still trying to get preggers."

"Damn it," Margot said. "Maybe we should spike her cocoa with birth control pills."

"Margot, honey, it's her life," Devon said, sitting up so he could take his mug. "You can't run everyone's."

"Right," she said, her hand on the doorknob. "I'll just focus on Daniel for now."

Eric's eyebrow rose.

"What?" she asked, really needing to leave.

"If you run his life, he'll run from you. We're just going to make a few cosmetic improvements, but that's it. You know what they say, the only time you can change a man is when he's in diapers."

"I'm not trying to change him. I don't even know him yet."

"Yeah, well, don't you be trying to make him into Gordon."

She almost spit out a smart-ass retort, but Eric wasn't that far out in left field. "Okay, I promise. To try."

The boys smiled. "Good girl," they said together, as if they'd rehearsed it for hours. "Now, get out of here. We'll see you when you get home."

WHILE SHE HAD BETTINA washing the turkeys and Rick sorting through thick bread slices, Margot busied herself with panicking. It was ten-fifteen, and the director was already hysterical. She'd tried to explain in the nicest possible way that it was costing more to shoot on a Saturday than it would have cost to hire two extra stylists, but he had dismissed her as an idiot, and demanded she get the turkey on the set in one hour.

One hour. She wasn't a magician. She only had two hands. Even with Bettina and Rick. But she couldn't waste her energy on the bastard out there. She had work to do.

Wash all the fat from the surface of the bird. Turn the turkey over and pull the skin tight. Sew it with needle and fishing line. Pull the neck skin tight and pin. Stuff the bird with wet paper towels. Tie the legs with thread. Roast it until the skin gets bumpy and dry, but it's still raw inside. Brush the bird with maloise, a heat-activated browning agent, then heat again. Get out the blowtorch and make small adjustments. Plate the bird, cover the paper towels with stuffing.

At the same time, of course, she had to make the turkey sandwiches. The roasted turkey was just a side note—the sandwiches were what Whompies sold.

But sandwiches were easier than whole turkeys, so Bettina and Rick would focus on those. She needed the stand-ins first. Then the real McCoys, and there wasn't time to do any of it.

One thing at a time. That's all. Work. Instruct. Don't freak out. And don't, can't, think about what's happening with Devon and Eric, and how Daniel is taking to his shopping expedition.

DANIEL STARED at the Hawaiian shirt, at the pineapples, the grass huts, the leis. "Are you kidding me?"

Devon looked at Eric. Eric looked back. They closed the dressing room door, leaving Daniel alone with…it.

THE BIRD WAS LOOKING GOOD, but Margot was still way behind. She tried to tell the director she couldn't be done so soon, but he didn't listen. So why should that surprise her? Had he ever listened to her yet on this shoot? Only threatened twice this morning to have her fired. She wanted to leave. Walk out and never look back. But she couldn't. She'd never quit in her life.

So here she was sitting at the big table with her paint-brush and her tears, and she focusing on the job.

"NO, NO. HERE'S WHERE I put my foot down." Daniel didn't care that he was speaking so loudly that the trans-vestite trying on weird hats at the mirror stopped to stare. They were still at Ricky's and he'd given in and given in, but this was too much.

For God's sake, when they'd asked him to come, he'd thought it was some kind of odd male bonding thing, that they'd buy whatever they needed to, and then go out for a beer or something. When it became clear they wanted to shop for clothes for *him*, he'd seriously considered hailing a cab, but they were his neighbors and all. So he'd been a good sport. More than a good sport. Which was about to end.

"Just try it," Eric said.

"You might be surprised," added his Doublemint Twin.

"I'm not wearing a bowling shirt from Grogan's Garage."

"It's very retro," Eric said, his hand going to his hip as he studied Daniel's bare chest. "Very cool."

Daniel brought the shirt closer to his body, not so he could put it on, but to hide. "It has a name stitched on it. Not mine."

"That's the cool part," Devon said.

"The name is Tiffany."

Devon sighed. Eric shook his head. Daniel shut the dressing room door.

IT WAS LUNCHTIME FOR THE CREW, but Margot didn't stop. She couldn't. The sandwiches that Bettina had made didn't work. The lettuce didn't match the Whompie's look. The turkey slices weren't thin enough. The tomato was already bleeding. So what else could she do but start again.

As Bettina cleaned up, Rick sorted through a row of lettuces while Margot sliced meat. Her phone rang and quickly she reached into her apron and shut it off. Then returned to slicing more turkey breast. This will end, she kept telling herself. Though the way she was feeling right now, she didn't know how she'd make it through the rest of the day. As if she had a choice

"JUST LOOK." Eric stepped back, clearing the way for Daniel. "One look. What can it hurt?"

Daniel didn't want to. He was tired. Cranky. He

wanted to leave. He had a pile of clothes at the counter and he wasn't sure he liked any of it. These two were merciless. They were like old ladies, clucking at him, adjusting things. Touching. Way too much touching. "No. I'm leaving."

"And we'll let you," Devon said, going for soothing, but it didn't work. "After you look in the mirror."

He didn't want to go out there to the three-way. Too many people. Men, women. Others. They all checked him out as if he were a slab of prime rib.

He sighed. Stepped out of the dressing room. Walked over to the mirror.

And was kinda surprised. The jeans were a little tight, but not as bad as he'd feared. The shirt was long sleeved, striped and also tight. As instructed, he'd left the bottom button undone, as well as the top two. Rolled up both sleeves, but just once. The material was silky, it felt good, which was important because it hugged him like a second skin. But overall, it looked, well, cool.

"You're a wet dream," Devon said.

Eric punched him in the shoulder.

"Someone else's wet dream," Devon amended.

"It's not bad," Daniel said, turning to his right. They weren't clothes he'd ever pick for himself. But it made his chest look bigger, his legs longer. He wondered what Margot would think.

As images formed of Margot's admiration, he saw another advantage to the tightness of the jeans. He might be getting a tad uncomfortable with the snugness and all, but there was so little give that nothing gave away his secret. Excellent.

On the other hand, getting a rise here in the gaymart wasn't his idea of a day at the park. "Fine," he said. "Let's get it up and go. I mean, get it and go. The clothes."

Eric and Devon high-fived. Devon waggled his eyebrows. Then they kissed.

Daniel had seen them do it before, and he was actually getting more comfortable with it. No big deal, right? They were in Chelsea, after all. Turning to go back to the dressing room, he heard a long, low wolf whistle. It was for him. The whistler was a buff guy in leather pants who reminded Daniel of Krycek from the *X-Files*. He wondered briefly if he should say thanks, but decided the best thing to do was forget about changing clothes and get the hell out of here.

MARGOT WAS STARTING TO FREAK. Not about her day. Well, not anymore. The moment she'd walked in her door, she'd had a good, old-fashioned hissy fit—screamed, yelled, threw pillows. Then she'd had a drink. A bubble bath with oodles of soothing aromatherapy. A good cry. Which had actually worked, up until an hour ago.

The boys were not home. It was nearly six-thirty, and they weren't home. None of them.

Damn it, why hadn't they come back? Or at least called. She'd tried to meditate, but that had been a bust. She'd called Devon and Eric's cell phones, which they hadn't answered. She'd whipped up a little dinner. And then she'd gathered all the supplies she'd need for Daniel. If he ever got here.

Her tummy fluttered as she thought about what the evening would bring. Not to mention the night.

Sex. Other stuff first, yeah, but after… Sex. Boffo-rama. The horizontal bop. The shizzle with fazizzle.

Which meant she'd be naked. Never a fun prospect, which now that she thought about it sucked. Men were never hesitant or embarrassed about being naked. Even if they looked like Jabba the Hut, they still just whipped it all off, proud as the Fourth of July. And what was with all the scratching?

She shivered at the image, needing to replace it with something far more pleasant. Daniel. Peeling off his slacks. His shirt tossed behind the couch. Her crouching next to it because she didn't want him to see her naked.

"Damn it!"

She went into the bedroom and slammed the door. Stared at herself in the mirror there. She had on black palazzo pants and a short red T. Her hair was down, clean. Her makeup minimal. She didn't look half-bad, even if she said so herself. So what was the problem?

Clothes. She had clothes on, and that was the issue wasn't it? Well, the opposite of the issue. Or something. It was after the clothing part that she tended to freak.

Daniel liked her. All she had to remember was the way he looked at her. She closed her eyes, picturing him the moment before he'd pulled her onto his lap. Oh, yeah. He had it bad.

He'd love her naked.

Her eyes opened. "Right," she said to the liar in the mirror. Then she got one of her diaphanous red scarves and placed it casually over her bedside lamp.

It was six-forty-five. If they didn't get here soon she'd—

The knock on the door prevented any potential mayhem. She hurried through the living room and swung it open. Standing before her was the hottest-looking man on the East coast. For a moment, she couldn't speak. Couldn't breathe. She just had to stare.

"Please tell me that's not a mask of horror."

"No. No, no, no. Oh, my God."

He smiled. And there it was. The Blush. God, he couldn't be cuter. Well, maybe if he took off the glasses, and his hair—it didn't matter, he was gorgeous. "You're stunning."

He rolled his eyes, but she could see he was pleased. And that he had two very large bags by his feet.

"Come in, and let me see."

He picked up the Ricky's bags and walked into her apartment. "So tell me something," he said, as he moved toward the coffee table. "When did you decide I needed a new wardrobe? Was it that first night, or did it happen sometime during the Moroccan feast?"

"Me? What did those two tell you?"

He obviously didn't buy the innocent act. In fact, he looked pretty pissed off. She borrowed his blush. "You're living in Chelsea now. It seemed appropriate."

"Was I really that bad?"

Glad to see the amusement in his eyes, she walked up to him. "No. Not bad at all. Just…"

"What?"

He was cute when he pouted. Major babe cute. "Just a little stodgy, that's all. And you're so very handsome, you deserved to have some clothes that showed you off."

With pursed lips and narrowed eyes, he stared at her

for a very long time. Then he sighed. "You make it very difficult to be mad at you."

She brushed his cheek with the back of her hand. "I practice."

"So you really think this works?"

She stepped away and looked him over from top to toe. The shoes could be better, but the jeans were snug-garific, and that shirt made her want to rub herself against him until he purred. "Works isn't near enough. You should be on the cover of *GQ*. And all the other letters. I'm serious. I bet every gay man at Ricky's was panting over you."

"Well, I did get whistled at."

"Oooh."

"And he was good-looking, too."

"I can see there'll be no living with you now."

He grinned.

"Show me the rest."

He bent down and pulled a shirt out of the bag. "Devon insisted on this one."

"Wait, wait, wait," she said, holding up her hand. Then she went to the couch and curled her legs underneath her. "On."

"What?"

"Put it on."

"Oh, no. I'm not going to go through that again."

"It's not a real fashion show unless you put them on."

He came over to where she was sitting. Right up to her, so that if she looked straight ahead she could see the detail stitching on his fly. "You have two choices. I can try on all the clothes. Or we can make out."

"Hmm," she said, putting her index finger to her chin. "Hey."

She grabbed him by the wrist, in a little replay of the other night, and pulled him down beside her. "I vote we make out."

"You're sure now? I have a pretty dashing pair of chinos in there." But then his lips were on hers and who gave a damn about clothes. Angling his head, he moved his mouth slowly, dragging it over Margot's, thrusting gently into the slick warmth within.

Long fingers laced through her thick hair, drawing her closer, while his tongue pushed back against her own, sliding, teasing. She moaned as he pushed harder, gentleness giving way to something darker. Just as she was beginning to lose herself in the sensation, someone banged at her door.

Daniel sat up, leaving her breathless. She could hear his rapid panting as he let go of her hair.

"Damn," she whispered.

He nodded as he swiped a hand over his face. "Expecting company?"

She shook her head, but called, "Come in."

It was Corrie. The minute Margot saw her, she knew that make-out time was over. Her best friend looked like hell. Her eyes were swollen and red, her skin blotchy from crying.

"I'm sorry, I didn't realize…" Corrie, sniffed. "I'll talk to you later."

Margot got up quickly. "No, it's okay. Get your tail in here."

Corrie hesitated long enough for Margot to grab

her hand and tug her inside. "I don't want to spoil anything."

"You're not," Margot said. "Daniel was just showing me some of his new clothes. You sit down and I'll make tea. Have you eaten?"

Corrie shook her head as she shuffled over to the other couch. She sat down with a sigh.

"Daniel, show her how beautiful you look. I'll be right back."

Daniel didn't move for a minute. He was taken aback by the sudden shift, his body still torqued from that kiss. But he could see Corrie wasn't in good shape. He leaned forward, put his elbows on his knees. "You okay?"

Another sniff, and Corrie brought some mottled tissue to her eyes. "No."

"What happened?"

"My husband, that's what happened. He's a bastard, and I don't know why I don't just walk out the door and never come back."

At a considerable loss, Daniel looked ferociously at his hands. "I'm sorry," he said, knowing it was hopelessly inadequate.

"Yeah, me, too."

Margot came back, and Daniel felt instant relief. She carried a tray with food and a ceramic teapot, three cups. He really wasn't much of a tea drinker, and thought of asking if she had any beer, but he kept his mouth shut for the moment.

"What happened?" Margot asked, as she put down the tray.

"He didn't come home until six this morning. Said

he was at the hospital, but he wasn't. He'd showered, his hair was still damp, for God's sake."

Margot sat down next to her. "Maybe he showered there?"

Corrie shook her head. "I know he was with her."

"Did you talk about counseling?"

"He told me I was paranoid. Asked me if it was that time of the month. God, I could just kill him when he does that."

"So what are you going to do?"

"I should leave."

"But?"

"Where the hell would I go? There aren't a lot of jobs out there for ex-pole dancers."

"You can stay here with me," Margot said.

Corrie shook her head. "Thanks, but being in the same building would be really tough. He'd bring her here, and then what? I'd cry myself to sleep on your couch every night?"

"But this is killing you."

"I'll talk to him again about counseling, when I'm not so emotional."

"That'd be good."

Corrie pasted on a weak smile. "So, Daniel. Tell me about your shopping spree."

"It wasn't much fun," he said, glad to change the subject, but wishing they could be discussing anything but him. "I'm not big on buying new clothes."

"You look really good in that," she said. "Very sexy."

He cleared his throat, not at all used to this attention. While it felt good, it also felt weird as hell. "Thanks."

"You haven't given him his haircut yet?"

Margot shushed her, but it was too late. Daniel sat back. "Pardon me? You want to cut my hair?"

Margot had the good grace to look chastened, but he could see her eyes still held plans. "Just a little. I'm pretty good at it."

"I think I've had enough changes for one day, but thanks anyway."

"She's being modest. She does Eric's and Devon's hair. Mine, too. And it always comes out great. You should let her. Really."

He didn't want to argue with Corrie, but jeez. He felt like one of those women on a TV makeover show. "Am I scheduled for any plastic surgery that I don't know about?"

Corrie laughed, and Margot came over to join him on the couch. She took his hand in hers. "Please don't be angry," she said. "I was just thinking how great you'd look with your hair all sexy and edgy. But if you don't want to…"

What did this woman do to him? Looking at her round, chocolate eyes, her full pouting lips, he felt at a total loss. "Margot—"

She smiled beautifully, her whole face coming alive. "Oh, thank you." She kissed him, swiping her tongue across his lower lip before she leaned back. "It'll be fun. I promise."

He grunted, not sure at all he liked where this was going.

8

MARGOT CLOSED THE DOOR, still feeling so bad for her friend. She hoped that Corrie and Nels could work it out, but she didn't have a good feeling about it. Nels could be a terrific guy, but his recent treatment of his wife made it hard to remember that. Corrie was a peach, and she deserved so much more.

"Hey," came a soft, low whisper just behind her. Daniel touched her shoulder, then moved in so she felt his whole body against her back.

"Sorry about that," she said. "I'm just so sad for her."

"Is there anything I can do?"

"Yeah, go beat up Nels."

"Okay," he said. Then he moved her aside and took hold of the doorknob.

She laughed. "You're too cute."

He turned around. "Too cute? I don't know that I want to be too cute."

"No?"

He shook his head. "I have to confess I'm feeling the need for beer and the WWF. Today has been pretty rough on my masculinity."

"Poor baby," she said, cupping his cheek. "Would

it help if I tell you I think you're a burning hunk of manliness?"

The left side of his mouth quirked up. "Yeah, I think it would."

She leaned toward him, rising on the balls of her feet so she could kiss him. Slowly, she brushed her lips against his, then teased him with gentle swipes of her tongue. He opened his mouth, and the gentleness disappeared as he took charge.

She shivered all the way to her toes as he crushed her mouth, as his tongue thrust inside her, dominant, demanding. His arms went around her back and he pulled her tight. She sank down, unable to keep her balance, as he showed her what was what.

His hands began to roam across the curves of her back, then down to the swell of her hips. He moaned as he reached lower, cupping her butt.

She loved kissing. Always had. But she'd never loved it more than this. He opened his mouth just enough, used his tongue like a finely tuned instrument; he even knew what to do with his teeth.

As he squeezed her flesh he moaned, and it made her all goose bumps and shivers.

But then his lips were gone. She looked up to see him staring over her head, his lips still moist, his eyes glassy. "What's wrong?" she asked, afraid to hear his answer.

His expression turned quizzical. "What is this?"

"Huh?"

"I'm sorry. It's not that I'm complaining, but since the moment I met you I feel like I've entered *The Twilight Zone*."

"Gee, thanks."

"In a good way."

"Not convinced. But I do kind of understand. It's all going pretty fast."

He let her go and her heart clenched. But all he did was walk back to the couch and stare at the bags on the floor. "I bought clothes."

"Yeah," she said, drawing out the word.

His gaze came up again. "I bought clothes I never would have looked at yesterday."

"I know."

"I'm actually contemplating letting you, a virtual stranger, cut my hair."

She nodded, not liking where this was headed.

"And basically," he said, his voice lowering to a velvet pitch, "all I can think about is how badly I want to sleep with you."

Heart kick-started, she went over and sat next to him on the couch. "And this is bad because…?"

"Because we just met."

"So?"

"I don't do things this way."

"Maybe you should."

"It's not me."

"Sure it is. You just haven't let yourself go before."

He shook his head. "I've never wanted to before."

"I repeat. This is bad because…?"

"It's not bad. Just weird."

"If it's any consolation, I'm pretty freaked out about it, too."

"Liar."

"I am. You think I try to seduce every man who moves into the building?"

"Most men who move into this building have different interests."

"Don't be so literal. My point is that this is a novel experience for me, also. I told you about my rings. When I barely knew you."

"You still barely know me."

"That's where you're wrong. I know you much better now."

"How's that?"

"Well, I know you're a terrifically good sport."

He kicked one of the bags. "Obviously."

"And you're amazingly kind."

His eyebrows came down in that way of his.

"The way you were with Corrie. And with Anya the other night. The way you look at me."

"That's not kindness, Margot. That's horniness."

She laughed. "Granted, that's there, too, but come on. You really are going to let me cut your hair, aren't you?"

"I might be convinced."

"Oh?"

His hand came up to the back of her neck where his cool fingers brushed against her skin. "About those rings…"

She smiled, wishing she had more of them, in far more interesting places. "Deal. I cut, you get to seek and find."

His grin was slow and wicked. "Where are the scissors?"

She held him down. "Wait."

"Why?"

"Because I think I need to just, I don't know, say this."

"Oh, God. You're not going to confess something really scary, are you?"

She shook her head. "No. At least I don't think so."

"What, for God's sake? I'm starting to worry."

She met him squarely on, not in the least sure that this wasn't a huge mistake. But she wanted whatever the hell was happening between them to be completely on the up-and-up. After a big intake of breath, she just went with it. "I'm thinking this is a sex thing."

His mouth opened, but nothing came out.

"Friendship, too. But, you know. Sex."

Again, he didn't speak.

"I mean, I don't want to give you the wrong impression. I'm not trying to make this more than it…is."

He cleared his throat. "I see."

She'd blown it. She'd meant to make him more comfortable, to assure him she wasn't trying to trap him into a relationship or anything. Not that that would be bad, but it wasn't the point. "Oh, shit. I wanted you to feel more comfortable, not less."

"I'm comfortable."

"Then why does your face look like that?"

He relaxed his furrowed eyebrows. But he was still looking at her as if she were from another planet. "You're an earthquake."

"I'm what?"

He paused for kind of a long time, then nodded. "No, that's about right."

"I'm an earthquake."

"The human equivalent thereof, yes."

"Meaning?"

"I can't stay on solid ground with you. I'm completely lost. Every step is a new adventure."

"And that's not good."

"I have no idea."

"I'm not sure how to react."

"Welcome to my world."

She petted his hair, loving the silky feel, knowing she was confusing the poor guy to distraction. "I'm sorry."

"Don't be. I think I needed this."

"I think so, too."

He laughed. A sharp bark that took both of them by surprise. "What am I going to be when you finish with me?"

"Finish? I haven't even started."

"Oh."

She leaned forward and kissed him gently. "Tell you what, you don't be scared, and I won't, either."

With his eyes still closed, he sighed resignedly. "I passed scared last Sunday."

"Cool."

His eyes opened again. Blue and serious as all get out. "So let's get the cutting over with, shall we?"

She stood, happy little trills running up and down inside her. "You're gonna love it."

He didn't say anything. Just gave her a polite and worried smile.

"Come," she said, taking his hand. She led him into the kitchen, where everything was already laid out. The chair, the plastic smock, the professional cutting scissors. Even a good standing light so she could see really well.

He sat down and gripped the bottom of the chair. She

didn't want to spook him any further, so she just put the smock around his neck, flaring it over his luscious body. Then she turned on the light.

One more thing, and she could begin. Standing in front of him, she bent and lifted his glasses from his face.

He squinted, and she melted a little. So beautiful. But he'd be even more so when she brought his Ricky Nelson do into the twenty-first century.

She put his glasses aside, and picked up the scissors.

Daniel closed his eyes. He had no idea why he was letting this woman cut his hair. No, cancel that. He knew exactly why. So he could get her into bed. No use denying that. He was still reeling from that little speech of hers on the couch. This was all about sex. And she'd said it apologetically. Boy was that a hundred miles off the mark.

He couldn't remember being given three wishes. Or even one. And still, here he was, with this amazing creature who was cutting off an alarming amount of hair. Oh well, what was a little hair when balanced against what was sure to be a mind-bending night?

The moment she'd opened the door, he'd forgiven her about the clothes. If she wanted him in a pink tutu, he'd… Well, he'd say no, but it would be difficult. She just had this way of turning him into a babbling idiot.

Probably because all his blood immediately rushed to his cock the moment she was near.

But since this was all about sex, that was okay, right? It was still difficult to wrap his head around it. Permission, granted. Sex. Friendship. Laughter. No commitments, no hidden strings, no obligations. Just sex with the most adventurous and interesting woman he'd ever met.

God, he loved Chelsea.

Her hand carded through his hair, lightly massaging his scalp, and he abandoned his thoughts. It was much better to just feel the magic spreading heat into every part of his body.

She brought her other hand into the act, and that was it, he was a goner. He had no idea if she'd finished snipping, and he didn't care as long as she didn't stop with the fingers.

"Oh, you like this, do you?"

He replied. Not so much in words as in a mindless groan.

She chuckled, and then her hands moved to the back of his neck. She rubbed for a while, liquefying his bones, then he felt a warm breath tickle his ear, teeth on his lobe. She didn't exactly bite, but it was close.

He officially hated his new jeans. They were killing him, strangling his favorite part. He wanted to just rip the damn things open, but he didn't want to scare the nice lady with the scissors.

"I'm almost finished," she whispered, after letting him go. "Patience."

"No one has that much patience, Margot."

She stood, picked up the scissors and went back to work. He shifted in the chair, but it didn't help at all. He listened to her humming, trying to figure out the tune, but he didn't recognize it. At least it had taken his thoughts from the discomfort between his legs. It was nuts, how she did this to him. It reminded him of when he was fifteen, and everything had made him hard. It didn't seem to matter if he was in his room alone, or in front of his class giving a report, something would set him off, and he'd stand up and salute. It didn't even have to be something sexy, either. He'd get riled over a word, a hint of cinnamon, the taste of ice cream. He'd worried for a long time that he wasn't normal, but things had settled down as he'd come into his twenties.

Well, so, he'd gone back in time. With Margot, that didn't surprise him much. Maybe she was a witch. That was actually a more likely explanation than that he was just infatuated with her.

Obsessed.

Way the hell in over his head.

"What's going on?" she asked.

His eyes opened, and he saw her standing in front of him. He felt as if he'd been awakened from a dream, but he knew he hadn't been asleep. "I'm getting a haircut. I think."

"That can't be it."

"What are you talking about?"

"You were blushing. Smiling. Uh, moaning a little."

"I was?"

She nodded.

He was in more trouble than he'd imagined. "What were you humming?"

"I wasn't humming."

"Yes, you were."

"Quit trying to change the subject."

"Ah, but I'm not. You were humming, and yet you can't remember. I was blushing, and I can't, either."

She narrowed her beautiful eyes. "Liar."

"Keep cutting."

She snorted, but it was actually pretty cute. And when she moved closer, he caught another whiff of whatever perfume she was wearing. He wasn't good with scents, one flower was pretty much like another to him, but this, he remembered. It was what she had worn the other night. Like everything else about her, it made him ache. He didn't have that much hair, what could be taking her so long?

She went back to work, and he focused on the snick of the scissors. He didn't want to close his eyes again, afraid that he'd reenter that fugue state she'd noticed. All he wanted was for her to hurry. And to adjust himself so that he wasn't being poked quite so hard by one particular button.

He shifted again on the chair, and she hissed. "Careful."

"Sorry."

Of course, now all he could think about was the button. Well, not the button so much as what it was pressing into. Damn it, he hadn't brought condoms. If she didn't have any, they were in serious trouble. Because he was quite sure he wasn't capable of waiting much longer.

Rings. She had rings. He tried to imagine where. Nipples? Even he heard this moan.

Margot, being made of ice, simply laughed. Again. "This is fun," she said.

"I'm so pleased I amuse you."

"Seriously. I've never enjoyed giving a haircut so much. Of course, you're wiggling like a ten-year-old, but so far I haven't made any bad mistakes."

His hand reached up to capture her wrist. "What kind of mistakes have you made?"

"None that you'd notice. Now, be a good boy and let me go. You want me to finish, don't you?"

"More than anything on earth. Tell you what, I'll give you my entire savings account if you just stop now."

She leaned down and kissed him hard on the mouth. But it was over before he could even react. "Down boy. Five more minutes."

"Two."

"Three."

"Deal."

"But you have to let go."

He did. Grudgingly. She snipped some more. It was hell. He didn't give a damn about his hair. She could have shaved his head and he'd have been happy, because it would be over. He sighed.

She patted his shoulder with her free hand. Snipped again.

He tried counting the seconds, but he couldn't concentrate. Finally, when he knew that three minutes had to be up, he reached for her hand again. Only, it was gone. She'd stepped back. "Are we done?"

"Not quite."

"You said three minutes."

"I didn't lie. I'm done cutting. But you have to wait just another few seconds."

"Why?"

"Because I have to get something."

She turned, and even while he was lunging out of his seat, she was gone. "Stay there," she called over her shoulder. "One minute."

"That makes four, damn it."

She didn't care. She just ran away.

He slumped back on the seat, but he'd had it. He struggled with the smock, finally figuring out where the end of the Velcro fastener was, and ripped the damn thing off. He tossed it over the table, covering the scissors.

He listened, waiting. But he didn't hear a thing. She'd gone to the back of the apartment, to either her bedroom or the bathroom.

He backed up a step. Maybe she had gone to the bedroom. Maybe she was getting ready for part two. She'd call his name, and he'd wander back, finding her on her bed, naked. Ready. Willing.

His hand went to his pants. He meant to just shift the damn button, but even after he did that, the relief wasn't enough. He was painfully hard. What he should do was open his fly, give the poor guy some air. Be completely ready when she asked him to join her.

Only, what if she wasn't there? What if she was doing something else entirely? Whatever it was, she'd better hurry because he couldn't stand this another minute.

MARGOT FOUND THE HAIR GEL at the back of her medicine cabinet. Her fingers were shaking as she picked it up, knowing that in just a few minutes, she and Daniel would be doing all kinds of wonderful things to each other. He'd really been patient while she'd cut his hair. She'd really been a horrible tease by taking her own sweet time.

But watching him writhe had been so excellent. She felt like standing on her tiptoes and yelling "I did that!" But she'd better get back to him. Whatever patience he'd had was surely gone by now.

With the gel in hand, she headed back into the kitchen. As she rounded the corner, she stopped dead.

Daniel, looking sexier than any human had a right to, was sitting quite still in the chair, the smock gone. His eyes were closed, and his hand was on the very noticeable bulge in his pants.

She shivered where she hadn't known she could. Squeezing her legs together didn't help. It was the most incredible thing she'd ever seen, and she'd never wanted a man so much.

She walked quietly into the room, stopping in front of Daniel. His eyes were still closed, and he was clearly so preoccupied he didn't even know she was there. Which would have been delightful if voyeurism had been her thing.

It wasn't.

She crouched before him. Lifted his busy hand and put the gel in his palm. "Do your own damn hair," she whispered as she reached for the top button.

9

DANIEL LOOKED AT THE JAR in his hand, then at the woman between his legs. The hair gel clunked as it hit the floor, but that was on some other planet where Margot wasn't unbuttoning his pants. Not having an easy time of it, either. He winced as she tugged and put his hands on hers. "Let me."

She slapped his knuckles. "I'll get it. Just lean back."

Like he was gonna argue. He leaned back as far as he could on the wooden chair, wishing this had happened on the couch, but not complaining. Oh, no. He spread his knees as far as they would go and her fingers brushed the side of his erection. He hissed and grabbed the bottom of the chair to hold himself steady. He just prayed she would get the buttons undone before it was too late.

"Tight suckers, aren't they," she asked as she struggled with button number two.

"Interesting choice of words," he said, his voice painfully drawn.

"Almost…" she whispered, slipping free button three "…got it."

He was going to die before she finished. At least he'd look good in his new clothes when they came and got the body. He cleared his throat. "Are you sure we shouldn't move—"

"We can do whatever you want," she said, smiling up at him. "After this."

He nodded, amazed his head still worked. He held his breath as she undid the last button. The relief from the pressure made him gasp. Her hand reaching into his boxer-briefs and wrapping around his flesh made him buck in the chair.

"Oh, Daniel," she said. "Such a big boy."

He tried to say thanks, but basically he just gurgled. He couldn't take it much longer. And when he felt her warm breath the sound turned to a groan that came from the edge of sanity.

He watched as she bent her head lower, and that pink tongue of hers came out, licking him, slowly, as if he were ice cream.

He touched the back of her head, not to hurry or press. For the contact. As amazing as this was, she seemed far away, and he needed to feel more of her.

She ran her fingers lightly up and down his shaft as she continued to explore him with her tongue. To see her like this, her eyes half shut, her cheeks warm and pink... Too much. He buried his fingers in her hair, wanting to pull her up into his arms, strip her naked and take her until they both crashed and burned.

But she wanted this. And he was way beyond denying her a damn thing.

MARGOT COULDN'T BELIEVE what she was doing. On her knees, in her kitchen, playing with Daniel like he was a great big lollipop. Every part of her felt on fire, wicked as hell. Dangerous. Well, she'd told him it was about sex, right? And sex it would be. Lots of it, in every way she could think of. It was like drinking the best wine, stealing the biggest piece of cake. Living out her every fantasy with her Man to Do.

He was salty and smelled like soap and man, which was an incredible scent. She licked him again, listened to the sound of his desperation, but she wasn't going to be hurried. This was heaven, freedom. And knowing he wanted more was ambrosia.

He pulled on her hair. It wasn't exactly gentle, but he didn't mean to hurt her. He couldn't help it, and she couldn't blame him. He'd been so patient. Staying in the chair while she took him all the way to the back of her mouth. So much coiled inside him that he was ready to explode, and still his fingers gentled and he stroked her.

It wasn't enough. The badness wasn't everything she wanted. She could have everything, couldn't she?

She licked him one more time, then she stood, using his knee to help her up. He watched her with wide eyes, scared, she imagined, that she'd decided to leave him, poor baby, in such a state. But when she was on her feet, she took his hands, and he stood, too. He leaned down and crushed her mouth with his. That strange power of his was back, she could feel it in his urgency, in his bruising hands on her shoulders, in the way he pulled her against him, made her feel what she did to him.

She gave as good as she got, kissing him with tongue and teeth. His hand moved under her T-shirt, to her back, and he touched her everywhere he could reach. Finally he was at the clasp of her bra and he fumbled, but only there. Not with his mouth, not with his plunging tongue. He pulled, tried to undo the damn bra, but it wouldn't budge, and then he just pushed it up, moved his hands, both of them, to the front where he practically ripped the thing off to get to her bare flesh.

He moaned when he touched her breasts. Squeezed her none too gently. He tore his mouth from hers and bent his head until his lips could replace his hand. He chuckled. "There's one," he whispered just before he licked the ring in her nipple.

She swooned for a moment. It had been a long time, and the last time had been a disaster from the word *go*. Which this definitely wasn't. He flicked the tip of her nipple with his pointed tongue, then did some swirly thing that made her forget how to breathe.

When he moved over to give equal time to her other nipple, she pulled her T-shirt and bra up and off, tossing it away so she was free to arch into his touch, to use her hands to run over his shoulders and his pecs.

Daniel moved up to the hollow in her throat, kissing, nibbling, exploring. His hands moved down to take off his pants, and she got the hint. Her fingers found the buttons on his new striped shirt and she undid those with a lot more finesse than she'd shown on his jeans, but there were fewer obstacles up there. Once it was open, she shoved it down his arms and tossed the garment behind her. He bent to rid himself of his pants, and when he stood up again, she was captivated by the gorgeousness of his chest.

"Holy shit," she whispered. And then she couldn't

help it, she had to lean forward and rub her cheek against him, hear his pounding heart, touch the dusting of dark hair.

His hands went to her pants, and while she didn't want to leave the comfort of his bare skin against her face, she stepped back and stripped the rest of the way, the better to feel all of him against her.

But before she could plaster herself to him, he held her back with outstretched arms and looked her up and down. She was naked in the kitchen with all that light pouring in from the window and the standing lamp, with no red scarf to make things hazy, and she didn't care at all, because oh, God, the way he looked at her. No one had ever looked at her with so much hunger.

"There's two," he said, touching the silver ring in her navel.

She kissed his chest again, reached down to take hold of his erection, but he grabbed on to her wrist and stopped her. She didn't understand. "Not yet," he said as he swung her around so her back was to the table. With both hands at her waist, he lifted her up on the edge of the table. Then, after a deep, breathless kiss, he touched her legs, and slowly spread them.

"Oh."

He smiled. Kissed her again. And then he went down.

Down to his knees, and being that he was tall and the table was kinda low, everything worked amazingly well.

He moved closer, breathed on the inside of her right thigh. She held still as he leaned in and kissed her gently, midway to the promised land, and then she felt his teeth, a little bite that made her start. Not painful, exactly, but exciting. More exciting was when he licked her right there, soothing the ache.

He continued exploring, nipping, licking, moving higher and higher up her thigh. After he got to the delicate skin where her thigh ended, he moved to her other leg, torturing her with his slow explorations.

She'd never thought about thighs as an erogenous zone. But oh, mamma, they were. She gripped the side of the table, watching him, his pleasure so evident in his careful ministrations. She wished she could see his eyes, but they were closed. His tongue so wet and talented, his teeth so even and sharp.

And then there was no more thigh to tease. He breathed on her aroused center and she shivered with the sensation. His smile was more than wicked as his thumbs moved to either side of her lips. He spread her open, and it was her turn to close her eyes. There was too much stimulation, she had to focus. She'd thought he was clever with her nipples, but she'd underestimated his talent. "Oh, God," she whispered as he did the most amazing things. The man knew how to take his time.

And how to drive her insane.

She grabbed his hair. Tried to. "Who the hell cut your hair so short," she said, but then she found her hold. She had to hang on tight because her whole body was shaking as he brought her closer and closer. Her legs stiffened, the muscles of her whole body tightening as she careened toward the edge of her orgasm. There was no way she could keep sitting up. Lying back on the cold surface of her Formica table gave her goose bumps on top of the ones already there.

And then he lifted her feet and put them flat on the edge of the table. She was spread before him like dessert, and he went right for the cherry.

While his tongue flicked, she felt his fingers at her entrance. Two fingers that slowly entered her warmth, and he pushed in and out, his speed increasing as he made her tremble.

She heard her voice from far away, crying out something, maybe his name, as she came. And came.

When she could think again, and see, he was gone. She struggled up, pushing with her elbows, letting her feet dangle once more, and then she saw him, and her mouth went dry.

Daniel was on her floor, sitting back on his haunches, his legs spread wide. He stared at her with smoky eyes, lids half closed. His lips were still moist.

Her gaze moved down past his strong jaw to the expanse of his incredible chest. Not much hair, just a sprinkling in the middle. His nipples were hard nubs, his stomach flat and perfect with an arrow of dark hair that led her eyes down.

He was still hard. His fingers brushed up the length of his cock. Slowly.

DANIEL WASN'T READY to end this, not nearly.

He could hardly believe what he'd done to her, how he'd let himself act without thinking, without what he'd always considered his ever-present voice of caution. There was no caution with Margot. His troublesome mind had shut off the moment she'd touched him, the second she'd gone to her knees, and he'd just acted. Done what he wanted, taken no prisoners.

Not like himself at all.

He watched her watching him. Unashamed that he was on such blatant display, that his need for her was completely out there. She, with her lush body, her curves and her softness, made him feel like a sybarite, like someone he'd never been before.

He wanted to touch every part of her, taste everything. To lock the doors and bar the windows and live in that sweet valley for the rest of time.

She smiled at him as her feet touched the floor. Walking to him slowly, she stopped when she was very close. Her gaze shifted between the hand at his cock and his face. Her breathing quickened, and he watched the rise and fall of her breasts. God, her breasts. They were big and full and so beautifully female he couldn't get enough of them. He stared on the silver ring in her right nipple, and his dick jumped.

If he kept this up, he was going to blow it.

"Bedroom?" she asked.

He nodded.

She held out her hand, and he stood up, his erection moistening the curve of her belly. He had to kiss her. No choice. She had the most incredible mouth. No hesitation, nothing demure. Just hot, lascivious pleasure.

Of course she had to break away first, because he would have stayed there for a hundred years. She led him through the living room to the door of her bedroom.

It was like her. Bigger than life; a four-poster bed

sheathed in white gauze, with pillows and pillows. The painting on the wall stopped him for a moment—large, lots of red, a naked woman sprawled on a chaise, looking satisfied and spent. Of course.

"You like it?"

"It's you."

"Not quite, but thanks."

He touched her again, cupping her breast, because he could. She laughed, bringing him closer to the invitation of her bed.

While he held her, she tossed pillows over the side, then pulled down the comforter, and then she turned, grabbing him by his shoulders, and guided him down.

When he lay flat, she joined him, curling between his arms. He found her lips once more, taking his time as he kissed her deeply.

Then she touched him, and the languor ended. All that pent-up energy centered right there, where her hand touched his flesh. A sharp, lacerating need cut through everything, and made him desperate for more.

He felt her mouth against the skin of his neck. Hot, wet lips trailing a path of agonizing pleasure. Her teeth nipped, her tongue licked and her hand started moving.

He rocked into the warmth, moaning, whimpering and finally, when he could stand no more, a growl that came from somewhere deep and feral.

She let go, broke away, and even as he reached for her he realized she was opening the bedside drawer. When she turned back, she brought the condom package to her teeth and ripped it open. After tossing the package, she sat up, leaned over him and with trembling fingers rolled the rubber over him. He'd never hated condoms more than he did that moment, because all he wanted was the feel of her with nothing in the way, but he couldn't ask her for that.

Once it was on, he thought she would lie back again, but she didn't. She pushed him so he was lying flat, and her leg swung over his hips.

He groaned, not even believing that she had known exactly what he wanted before he knew he wanted it. But her on top...so he could watch her, drink her body in while she rode him. He knew he wasn't going to last long, and he felt an apology rise, but when she captured him with one hand to hold him steady, he couldn't speak.

She lowered herself with agonizing slowness. Inch by aching inch he entered her heat. Tight, wet, more than he could stand.

He bucked but her hands held his hips down. He growled again, but she only laughed at his distress. He watched her body lower farther, watched as her breasts rose and fell, as he was swallowed by the voluptuous creature that had turned him inside out.

Finally, after an eternity of anticipation, he was buried to the hilt, and it was the most intense thing he'd ever felt. He reached out to touch her, his fingers unsteady, his breathing rough and harsh.

She leaned slightly forward so he could cup her breasts, and then she moved. Her hips lifted, bringing him the friction, until it was just the tip of him inside her. Hesitated. Moved down again until he was home.

He couldn't take the slow pace, needed more, now, but she held him steady, torturing him with every aching rise and fall. "Please," he whispered, knowing he was begging, not giving a damn.

With a wicked and knowing smile, she granted his wish. She moved faster, rising and falling, building in speed. Her hands left his hips, and he was free to move with her, against her, until it was everything in the universe, the pulse up and down, slamming into each other, their voices loud and inarticulate. He grabbed on to her hips and with one violent thrust he exploded, and there were fireworks of white and red behind his eyes and spasms racked his body while his heart pounded in his chest.

He collapsed, dragging in a breath that burned his throat. When he opened his eyes, she was just watching him, her mouth slightly open, her head tilted to the side. "You're so beautiful," he said, not surprised at the gravel in his voice.

"You are," she whispered back.

"You're too far away," he said, taking her arm.

She spread out next to him, and he hated to disturb the moment at all, but there were things to do. Thankfully, they didn't take long and then they were together under the comforter, and he wallowed in the feel of her body pressed against him.

He smiled at her, loving the way her hair spread out across the white of her pillow. "Now that's what I call a great haircut," he said.

She laughed, but as she studied him, she grew serious. Her hand came to his face where she traced his jaw with her finger. "My goodness," she whispered. "Who knew?"

He shook his head. "I've never met anyone like you. And when I'm with you, I'm…"

"You're what?"

"Not me."

She frowned. "Don't you think that maybe you're more you?"

"Perhaps."

"Whoever you are, you're amazing."

"Thank you. And may I return the compliment?"

"You may."

He couldn't hold his head up any longer, so he let it drop. The scent of her hair teased him with strange fruit. He sighed, deeply content.

"Here's the thing," she said.

He was instantly concerned. He looked at her, not wanting to hear that something was wrong. Please, God, don't stop this just when it was beginning.

"I've got to get something to drink."

He laughed.

"What?"

"Nothing. I'll go. What would you like?"

"There's iced tea in the fridge."

"Anything else?"

She shook her head. "Nope. I'm fine."

He lowered his lips to hers. Kissed her there, then on the tip of her nose. "Yes," he said. "You are fine. In fact, you're perfect."

10

MARGOT WATCHED HIM SLEEP. They'd both crashed after they'd had some liquid nourishment, but she'd gotten up about ten minutes ago, and kept very still while she studied him.

Her body had yet to completely calm down from the festivities, and that was okay by her. She remembered her shattering orgasm and shivered again. He was stunning. And it scared her to her toes.

Who was this guy? He couldn't be as good as he seemed. No one could. Bright, funny, successful, kind and hung like…well, at least she could verify that last thing with complete confidence. As for the rest? She wanted to believe what she saw was what she got, but how could it be?

She remembered too clearly what she'd thought about Gordon in the beginning. They'd met at a bookstore, at a reading of one of her favorite authors. Gordon had been one of the few men in attendance. She'd kept staring at him. The man was a babe. Major babe. Long dark hair pulled back in a ponytail, dark and dangerous looking, all sex and leather. When he'd approached her, out of all the women there, she'd been flattered beyond words. When he'd asked her for coffee the next night, she was a goner.

She didn't even like to admit it to herself, but on their second date, she had been already planning the wedding. Yeah, he'd been between jobs, but he was so smart and smooth, she knew he'd get one soon, and besides, they'd have gorgeous babies together. She'd had everything worked out within weeks. Where they'd get married, which rabbi would officiate, who would cater. So the first time that he'd stood her up, she hadn't worried at all. By the fourth time, she'd been so deeply enmeshed in her fantasy that she just couldn't admit the truth, even to herself.

Finally, when he'd borrowed all the money he could from her, when she'd found out he was using her apartment to meet up with his drug connections, she'd had to get real. She'd kicked him out on his high, tight ass, and told him never to darken her door again.

He'd called, though, several times, and each time, it had nearly killed her. Not because of what she'd lost, but because he was a bastard, because of what a fool she'd been.

She couldn't do it again. Wouldn't. That's why all she could be to Daniel was a friend with benefits. A Man to Do. It was ridiculous to think of it as anything more, anyway. Regardless, this time, she wasn't going to lie to herself. She wasn't going to pretend about anything.

Sex, fun, friendship. She'd give herself as long as it took to understand the man. To find his flaws. To let him see hers. She'd finally learned her lesson about jumping into the deep end without checking for water.

He was the most delectable creature she'd ever seen, but she hardly knew him. She knew really good stuff, like the fact that he had the most adorable mole on his tush, but she didn't know his dark side.

Everyone had one. Without exception. Some were just darker than others. She prayed his was pale gray.

DANIEL STOPPED just before he got to his private office. It was the wolf whistle that did it, and this time it wasn't a gay man doing the whistling. It was Jill, the receptionist. He knew that because she was the only one around.

He turned slowly, still thinking he was nuts, that she'd whistled at something else, that it was a joke. But then he saw her sitting behind the huge oak desk, and her smile was all the evidence he needed. Her grin was wide, her eyebrow arched, and there was unabashed leering in her gaze. Which was bizarre, because Jill was the definition of prim and proper.

"Nice shirt, Daniel," she said.

He should have worn his jacket, not flung it over his shoulder. "Thank you."

"And that haircut. Very hip."

He took a step back, quite shocked by this new side of Jill. She was a really nice woman in her late thirties, all business, all the time. He'd never, not ever…

"I'd like to meet her sometime," Jill said, and then she answered the phone.

He hurried into his office and shut the door behind him. If he'd known this would have happened, he would have moved to Chelsea years ago.

But Jill's reaction, while surprising, wasn't a major deal. Margot was.

He sat down, leaned back in his leather chair and put

his feet up. He should be working, but screw it. He wanted to think. The weekend had gone by in a blur, what with staying up most of the night on Saturday, not getting out of bed until four on Sunday, and then the tenants dinner, he'd hardly slept. They'd both decided not to spend the night together last night, being reasonable people who had to get up early, but when he'd gone to kiss her good-night, that good intention had gone straight to hell.

More like heaven, in truth. He couldn't get enough of her. When he was with Margot, he felt freer than he'd ever imagined possible. She made him reckless, daring. Knowing that there were no strings gave him a comfort he'd never had with another woman.

With Emily, as with every other relationship, the first date had been a sort of job interview. The tacit agreement was that things would lead to things, ending in marriage, if all the pieces fit together. The contract was always on the table, waiting for signatures, and he'd never even guessed it had been such a burden.

But now that it wasn't there, he could see it all. Especially with Emily. She'd weighed his future at the firm, his family history, his potential as a father. To say it had put a pall over things wasn't exaggerating.

To be honest, it wasn't all her fault. He'd done the same with her. Because he was just past thirty, and it was the appropriate time for him to get married. To begin the next phase of his life.

But he didn't want to. Not yet. Not when he could have this much fun.

Margot was the perfect woman. She liked her job, her

friends, her busy, full life. He felt lucky that she had the time to spend with him, but he had to get it together, and not take advantage. He knew what this job meant to her, and he didn't want their fun to get in the way.

On the other hand, she was damn hard to resist. Even now, after that mind-blowing weekend, he wanted her. He could practically feel the softness of her skin, smell the fruity scent of her hair.

Okay, not a good thing to think about when anyone could walk in his office at any time. Now was for work, later was for play. And make no mistake about it, he had every intention of playing as hard as he could.

"MA, I CAN'T TALK."

"What's wrong?"

Margot walked off the set to the women's rest room, where she closed herself in a stall and locked the door. She turned up the volume on the phone, and slumped against the wall. "Everything."

"That's not possible," her mother said. "Start at the beginning."

"I don't have the people I need to do the job properly, so I'm constantly chasing my own tail. And the director hates me. He hasn't said one nice thing to me. Ever."

"You have more talent in your little finger than he has in his whole *tuches*. Have you told him about what you did for *Bon Appétit?*"

"He doesn't care. This is television. And it's Whompies, and they want things a certain way. Unfortunately, their way sucks."

"Well, show them how it should be done."

"That's just it, I can't. I don't have the time or the resources. It's just…"

"What, baby?"

"I don't know if I have it in me to do this."

"So quit. What do you need this headache for?"

"Ma, I appreciate it, but we've gone over this before. Remember the five-year plan?"

"I know, sweetheart, and I believe in you. Maybe this isn't the right five-year plan, have you thought about that?"

"A billion times…this morning."

"So what are you going to do?"

"I'm going to do my job to the best of my ability."

"You sure?"

"I have to give this everything I've got, Ma, or I'll never forgive myself."

"You won't have to. In the end, they'll beg you to stay."

"You have to say that, you're my mother."

"True. But I also happen to believe it."

Margot smiled, and for the first time since she'd gotten to work she didn't feel like shooting herself. "Ma, I love ya. I gotta go—"

"Wait. Tell me about this boy."

"He's not a boy, mother. He's an architect."

"Is he Jewish?"

"No."

"Dump him. Immediately."

"I repeat, I love ya, but I have to go. I'll call you later." Margot switched off her phone before her mother got started. Then she went to the sink, washed her hands, straightened her apron and steeled herself to go make tacos.

Perfect tacos. Whompie tacos.

She wouldn't think about Daniel even once. Not until lunch, at least.

THE TACOS WERE the simplest thing she'd been faced with, which was more of a relief than she cared to admit. She'd put Bettina on the task of frying up the shells, and Rick was shredding the lettuce. She'd made up several batches of ground beef, and was now draining them of any remaining fat. She'd wait till the last second for the tomatoes, and the taco sauce.

Now that she had a minute, she started the deep fryer again, and pulled out several bags of frozen fries. She'd fry them briefly, then make her selection. She had her small paintbrushes and food coloring ready, along with her blowtorch and toothpicks. While she was doing the fries, she'd have Bettina and Rick work on the milk shakes. Those were easy, too. Maybe she'd actually get through today without being yelled at. Too much.

DANIEL WAS WAITING at her door when she got home, and she'd never been happier to see another human.

"Uh oh," he said, pushing himself off the wall. "I was going to suggest we go out for dinner, but from the looks of things, I'm thinking delivery Chinese and a back rub."

She sighed as she fell into his arms. "You, my good man, are a *mensch*, you know that?"

"I aim to please."

She laughed, and it felt damn good. She kissed him

square on the lips, then opened the door. He followed her in and went right to the phone. "Tell me what you want."

"You. À la carte."

"Chinese, woman. Food."

"Don't talk to me about food ever again." She threw her purse on the couch. "I hate food and all food-related industries! Sweet and sour chicken, spring rolls and fried rice."

He grinned and dialed Won Ton Charlie's, which was only a block away.

She went straight to her bathroom to start her shower. She smelled fried and felt toasted, and only the thought of Daniel made her want to live another day. Listlessly, she took off her dress, pulled the pins out of her hair, and then reached back to undo her bra.

His knock stopped her.

"Come in," she said.

"Need someone to wash your back?"

She nodded, her hands dropping to her sides.

"Come here," he said, holding out his arms.

She fell against him, burying her head in the crook of his shoulder. "I am constitutionally incapable of making a Whompies taco."

"I don't believe you."

"Believe it. I made so many of them, I never want Americanized Mexican food again. The director hated them all. The shells were too dark, the lettuce too light, the meat not juicy enough. The only thing he liked all day was the milk shake. Anyone can do a milk shake, Daniel. The grips can do a milk shake."

"It'll be better tomorrow, I promise."

"Only if they take tacos off the menu."

He hugged her tight, then he undid her bra. "Shower now, talk tacos later."

Margot looked up into his gorgeous face. "You're too good to me."

"I know. It's a flaw. One I've learned to live with. Now come on, drop those panties."

"Yes, sir," she said, and she obeyed instantly, not feeling in the least weird that she was all naked and he was still dressed in work clothes. "What about you?"

"I don't wear panties."

She waggled her eyebrows. "Ever want to?"

He laughed. "Not my kink."

"Hmm. What is your kink?"

"Too numerous to mention. But one involves a beautiful woman in a shower."

"How long until we have food?"

"Twenty minutes."

She stepped under the water, but didn't close the curtain. "Then you'd better hurry."

He did a miraculously fast striptease, one that frankly could have used more finesse, but who was she to complain when the outcome was a joy to behold. And ooh, when he turned to join her she saw he was, indeed, very happy to see her.

She stepped back to give him room, and he climbed in real close. Yummy close.

He bent down to kiss her and it was like standing in a rainstorm. A really bad rainstorm, because one of the great things about this building was the water pressure. While she loved the kiss, the drowning part wasn't her favorite. She took his hips and moved him out of the direct flow.

"Better," he said, his lips still against hers.

"Much."

"How's this?" she asked.

He got really pink. "Well, it's a little difficult to reach the shampoo."

"I think you should try," she said, squeezing just a bit.

Daniel cleared his throat. "Definitely not getting the shampoo."

She sighed dramatically. "If you didn't want me to play with it, why did you bring it into the shower?"

"It comes attached."

"Yeah, but did you have to bring it fully inflated?"

He laughed, but then he got her back by sneaking his fingers below the equator.

"Whoa, cowboy," she said, "I thought we were getting clean in here."

He reached up, grabbed the bar of soap, and came right back down.

She nodded happily. "Excellent. Wash away."

He did. Very carefully. So carefully, that she had to hang on to the showerhead so she didn't fall down. Then, with only moments to spare, she had to return the favor, and of course they had to wash up again. But it was worth it.

Just as they stepped out of the shower, there was a knock on the door. Naked, still wet, Margot looked up into Daniel's very shocked face. "Go get it."

"I…it's…" He looked at his clothes on the floor, all in a jumble.

She should have let him off the hook. She had a robe on the other side of the door. But it was so much fun watching him dress as if the house was on fire. Not just his pants. Oh, no. His shorts, pants, socks, shirt, shoes, and jacket. By the time he left to get the Chinese food from the delivery guy, Margot couldn't breathe she was laughing so hard.

His expression as he left her, still quite naked, in the bathroom, was something she'd remember forever.

DANIEL FINISHED HIS BEER and put the bottle on the kitchen table. His favorite table ever. Margot had already finished hers and had gotten up to rinse the silverware. The evidence of their Chinese takeout was a jumble of boxes in the trash. He stopped her as she was coming away from the sink. "Would you like to come to my place?"

She waggled her eyebrows, and stroked a pretend mustache. "Why, to see your etchings?"

He laughed. "Actually, yeah."

She sat down next to him, crossing her legs and tucking her thick white robe over her knees. "Really?"

"There are some things I'd like you to see."

"Does this have anything to do with your legendary list of kinks?"

"Some people might think so, but I have the feeling you won't."

"Well, now I'm pleased and upset all at once."

"Upset?"

"I was looking forward to hearing about your, you know."

"Okay, I promise. I'll give you some strong hints. But let's go to my place before I lose my nerve."

She looked at him curiously as she stood. "I'll be dressed in a minute."

After she left, he sat back, looked at his hands. He hadn't planned on inviting her over. They stayed here, where she was comfortable, and when it was time for work, he went home and changed. Frankly, he didn't care where they got together, so long as there was a bed involved. But that's not why he wanted Margot to come over.

He'd never shown anyone his personal drawings. The ones he did when he was upset, or when he was so fed up with the old-fart designs he did day in and day out at work. These were his secret, and he'd always liked it that way.

But he wanted Margot to see them. A lot. He wanted to see the expression on her face when she saw what he'd done. She'd asked about kinks, and while this probably wasn't in any sex manual, it was an aberration.

His family would have been appalled. They didn't go for any of this futuristic stuff.

Emily would have been shocked, too. She'd approved of the art he had, and for his birthday, she'd bought him a signed Rockwell. Because that's all he was to her. Old-fashioned, conservative, good family, strong ties to the community. Yeah, that's all he'd been to everyone, including himself.

He looked down at the shirt, the one he'd never have bought in a million years. Maybe that's not all he had to be.

"Okay, I'm ready."

She'd put on some jeans and a loose silky shirt, pulled her hair back in some enormous tortoiseshell thing. Maybe, after the etchings, they would get back to that conversation about kinks.

He'd have to come up with something interesting. 'Cause he sure as hell wasn't about to tell her the truth. A man had to draw the line somewhere.

11

MARGOT TRIED TO IMAGINE WHAT Daniel was about to
show her. He'd said etchings, which made sense since he
was clearly artistic in an architectural sort of way. Maybe
he wanted her to see the drawings of his buildings, which
was cool. She wanted to know that part of him.

They left her apartment and went to the stairs instead
of waiting for the slow elevator. Once inside the stairwell, Daniel put his hand on the small of her back in a
very protective gesture that made her chest tighten. She
still hadn't seen the wrong thing about him, and her step
slowed as it occurred to her that going to his place might
be too revealing.

"You okay?"

She nodded and smiled as they reached the second-
floor landing.

He led her down the short hall to his place and un-
locked the door. When she walked inside, she wasn't
surprised by how neat the apartment was. Daniel was a
meticulous man in so many ways.

The walls remained off-white, the floors a dark hardwood, as they'd been when Seth Boronski lived there,
but the furniture transformed the place. And not for the
better. Everything looked as if it was right out of the

Boring Shopper catalog. Oak coffee table, beige fabric couch, sturdy bookcases. The problem was there was no Daniel anywhere. None of his humor, his passion, his soul. "It's nice," she said, not knowing what else polite to say.

"It's comfortable. Can I get you something to drink?"

She leaned over and kissed his cheek, her lips tingling as they brushed his five o'clock shadow. "No, I'm fine."

His gaze raked her face and he nodded solemnly. "You're more than fine."

Another strange twist in her chest. "I've got my issues."

"Don't we all. My friend Bill says the key to healthy relationships is to find someone with compatible insanities."

"I can deal with that."

"Speaking of which, come on." He took her hand and led her to his bedroom door. They had the same floor plan, so she knew where everything was, but the similarities ended there. Where her place was lively, exotic and colorful, his was subdued and practical. The little she knew of his background seemed steeped in a kind of reticence she couldn't understand. Perhaps because her family was so exuberant. Russian Jews who'd come to America after the First World War, they'd always been loud and obstinate and free with their laughter and their love. She was lucky that way, although she hadn't realized how fortunate until she'd reached adulthood.

Daniel had spoken of the quiet meals at his home, where the cutlery had done all the talking. How anger had been a thing to mistrust and emotions weren't shared.

He escorted her to his large desk at the back of the bedroom. But first, she checked out his bed. It was an attractive antique bed, large, heavy, but it made her think of lonely New England nights instead of passionate sex.

"I do a lot of work here," he said, grabbing her attention once more. "But this is also where I get creative."

"Oh?"

"You have to understand this is just for fun. I'd never do anything with this. I've never even shown anyone my stuff before."

Despite his claim, his orderly drafting table held only tidy pencils and odd-looking rulers. "Well?"

"Okay," he said, as if he'd just this second decided to go through with it. He reached beside his desk and pulled out a large dark leather portfolio which he put down on the table and unzipped slowly.

He pulled out a stack of drawings, and her eyes widened as she caught a hint of the top one. He laid them down carefully, then took a half step back.

She moved so she could see the drawing. It was a building, but not anything she'd seen in real life. Alive with color and grace, line and texture, it looked futuristic, but not in the least bit campy. More like something that would be on the cover of *Architectural Digest 2050*.

It was the antithesis of everything she saw in his apartment. The walls were eggplant, the molding had a hint of art deco, but not quite. Stained glass windows that had nothing to do with old churches were a perfect counterpoint to the curved roof. "Daniel, this is incredible."

"You don't think it's silly?"

She whirled to look at him, and he was such a puppy

that she wanted to hold him forever. "It's fantastic. Gorgeous."

"I read a lot of science fiction, and I fell in love with *Metropolis*, you know the Fritz Lang movie, when I was a kid. I devoured comic books. Not so much the stories as the astonishing artwork, like from Frank Frazetta, but I didn't want to go that far out there, so I combined some of the classic elements of Gothic and Greek architecture with the concepts of fluidity and motion and, well… There are more."

She knew this was a big thing. Very big. His voice alone, with its almost tremor told her that. This was the heart of Daniel, and she felt humbled that he was offering it to her. This was the man he deserved to be, not the stick-in-the-mud that had taken him hostage.

She sat on his stool and got comfy. No rushing through this for her. "You know, I would like something to drink," she said.

"I'll be right back," he said.

"Take your time. I'm going to take mine."

Daniel went to the kitchen and looked at his beverage selection. Beer it was. He got two bottles, and headed back to his room.

He was inordinately pleased that he'd shown Margot his drawings. He'd watched her face carefully, and no way she could have feigned her delight. Damn, he knew it. Knew she'd see the beauty of the untraditional. Hell, that was what he liked about her, that she wasn't a cookie-cutter copy of the women in his life. Even Gretchen, who'd gone through her rebellious stage in her teens had come around to his parents' attitudes and standards. Nobody rocked the boat in the Houghton clan.

He could imagine his father's face if he ever got a load of his drawings. The thin line of his mouth, the disgust in his eyes. Not that Daniel had ever truly rebelled. He'd gone to Rutgers because his father had, but also because it was a fine school. No regrets there. And he had refused his father's offer to join his firm. But that's about as far as he'd gone.

It's not as if he had regrets. Not many, at least. He liked what he did, despite the fact that his designs were more nineteenth century in style than contemporary. It would be more fun if there were a broader range of options, but he had all the security he could ask for.

He walked into the bedroom to find Margot still bent over his work. A lock of hair had come out of the clasp and hung down her back. He loved it when she let it loose so he could run his fingers through the incredible silk of it. Everything about her was soft and enticing. Just thinking about her skin made him want her, want to pull her on top of him so he could feel everything from chest to toe.

He was glad now that he'd given in to the oddness of shopping with her friends. He doubted he'd wear any of his other new purchases to work. Jill's reaction, while it had pleased his sartorial self, was a clear indicator that the new and different stood out too much for Kogen, Teasdale and Webster.

But he'd wear them when he was with her, and that was the point, wasn't it? Making Margot happy. Such a different experience. Not that he'd wanted Emily to be unhappy, but he'd never felt this strong desire to please her. Margot brought out a lot of new things in him.

"Daniel."

He walked to the table, handed her the bottle of beer, which she set aside.

"This house is the most beautiful thing I've ever seen. I want this house."

He felt his chest swell as he looked at her, her enchantment written all over her face. "I'll build it for you."

"Really? You can make this? Now?"

"Of course. There's nothing so radical that it couldn't be built. All of the structures I design have a sturdy basis in design principles and construction capacity."

"Then why aren't they being built?"

"Other than you and me, I'm not sure anyone would want them. In case you haven't noticed, they're a bit iconoclastic."

"So? There are tons of iconoclastic buildings out there. There's even a show on HGTV that's all about extreme houses."

"That's true, but this is really just a hobby. I told you. Just for fun."

"Well, it's a damn shame, because I bet there are tons of people who'd love to own one. I'm not kidding, either. I figure a few years from now, you're the man who's building my dream house."

"In Chelsea?"

"Nope. I'm not sure where. Maybe Long Island. Or upstate. Somewhere I can have a lot of land."

"Done," he said. "By then, I'll be a partner and they won't be able to say boo about my personal projects."

She touched his cheek with the cool palm of her hand. "Deal."

He leaned over and kissed her.

She pulled back until their lips were barely touching. "Thank you."

"You're welcome."

"Want to fool around?"

"Always."

"But it can't be an all-nighter. Sleep is imperative."

"I concur."

"Back to my place?"

"Take your beer."

Margot did, and she rubbed his back as he carefully put away his work. This was the best he'd felt in years. And what a difference from the way he'd felt most of the time living in Greenwich.

The only thing he'd really looked forward to had been his hobby. Reading his science fiction and fantasy books and designing his dream structures. Not that he'd hated everything else. There were the guys, always good for a laugh. Yeah, they'd gone to Knick's games and shot pool and even some high-brow stuff, but basically when he got together with the guys he was back in college. He didn't have such fond memories of dating, although he'd done his share. No woman had come close to Margot. Not by a mile.

"Ready?"

Daniel realized he'd been staring at nothing for a while, lost in thought, and he happily returned to the present. And she was a present, wasn't she? A gift he got to open over and over. "Yeah, let's go get naked."

"Shouldn't we wait till we're in my apartment?"

"Chicken." He laughed, then got a little worried. "You would do something like that, wouldn't you?"

"I'd have to be a lot drunker, but yeah, I might."

"I see."

She ran her hand lower down his back, landing right on his butt. "I think there's something you forgot to tell me."

"I can't think of anything."

She pinched him, hard. "Ow."

"Come on, slick. One kink, and you'd better make it juicy."

"Okay, okay. But let's get out of here first."

Her hand left his ass as she walked into the living room, and he kind of missed it.

When they got to her apartment, Margot stopped him just inside the door and pushed him against the wall. She gave him a blistering kiss, and while he was still catching his breath she whispered, "Strip."

He obeyed, as quickly as he could, while she did the same, tossing clothes all over the couch and the floor.

When they were both down to shoes, she stopped his forward momentum by putting a hand on his chest. He stood very still as she eased herself to her knees, her mouth inches away from his rapidly rising erection. Her gaze stayed level as she slipped his shoes off his feet, then eased his socks off. By the time he was barefoot, he thought he might come if she breathed in his direction.

Surprisingly, he didn't. Not even when she swiped the head of his cock with her languid tongue. No rush, just a nice slow lick.

"Oh, God."

"No, just me."

He took her by the elbows and brought her up into his arms where he kissed her until the fabric of time ripped, until the whole universe was centered right there in her lips, in the arch of her breasts against his chest.

When she finally pulled back it was for an excellent cause. "Bedroom," she said, her voice filled with promise.

They hurried, Margot kicking off her shoes as they went so by the time they'd reached the bed she could fly under the comforter and beckon him to join her.

He turned off the light first, because he didn't want to bother later. Then he was next to her, his body pressed against her soft, velvet flesh.

He went to take her mouth again, but she stopped him with her finger on his lips. "Tell me."

"Now?"

She nodded.

"Can't we do this later?"

"You'll fall asleep."

"Weren't you there when we had the whole 'sleep is imperative' conversation?"

"So you should probably get to talking."

He closed his eyes, willing his dick to calm the hell down. "A kink, right? What if I told you I was so utterly banal that I have none."

"I'd say you were lying."

"How about we negotiate?"

"Fine," she said, but she raised the stakes immediately by wrapping her hand around him.

"No fair."

"Never said I was."

"I can't think of a damn kink."

"Shh, we don't need the neighbor's opinion. If you can't think of a kink, which, by the way, I find very suspicious, then tell me your first sexual fantasy. The very first time you ever had a thought that made all your engines fire."

"I don't remember."

She squeezed him in a way that was not altogether pleasant.

"Okay, okay." He took in a breath, and tried to concentrate on his words instead of her hand. "I guess it was when I was twelve or so. I had this fantasy that I had this dungeon. It was a secret dungeon underneath my bedroom."

"Ooh, I like that." She showed her approval by stroking him lightly.

"I had these women there. In chains."

"What women?"

"No one I knew personally. My friend Jordie Kellog had swiped some of his older brother's *Playboys* and we'd take turns reading them."

"The articles?"

He leaned up on his elbow. "*Playboy* had articles?"

She laughed and stroked him again. "Go on."

"There's not much more," he said, falling back down to rest his head on the pillow. "They were just there. My captives. And well, that's when it got fuzzy."

"What do you mean, fuzzy? How can women in chains be fuzzy?"

"I wasn't just twelve, I was an incredibly naive twelve. So I would imagine I had them down there, and nobody knew but me. And I did…stuff."

"What stuff?"

"You're not getting it. There wasn't anything else. It was just, I don't know. Stuff."

She studied him in the dim light from the window. "Oh, my God, you're serious."

"Oh, yeah. Nothing but the truth, so help me."

She giggled. Burrowed her head against his shoulder and shook with laughter. If it hadn't been so pathetic, he'd have laughed, too.

Finally her shaking stopped and he felt a gentle kiss on the side of his chest. "If I ask you nicely, will you do…stuff to me?"

"I was planning to."

"Even if I'm not in chains?"

He rolled far enough away that they weren't touching. Taking both of her hands in his, he pulled them up over her head, holding them steady. Then he took her in, from the desire in her eyes to the way her breasts lifted so sweetly, to the unmistakable thrust of her hips off the bed. "You remember that talk we had about kinks?"

She trembled. Before she laughed. But then she wasn't laughing, she was straining against him, trying to escape his hold, only he tightened his grip and he could feel her heat, feel her stretch her muscles, point her toes, and there was nothing fuzzy about a single thing.

12

To: The Gang at Eve's Apple
From: Margot
Sub: Yowza!
Dear Fellow Travelers:

I'm still riding the bliss train in a first-class compartment. Well, sexwise, not workwise. Work is actually sucking quite a bit. I thought it would be so easy to do this job. Just give the nice people what they want. I didn't factor in that they wouldn't give me enough people, or enough time, or that the director would be such an utter ass. So I kill myself to get it all done. And they hate it. So I go back to the kitchen and try again. It's far more torturous than it sounds, and I'm alarmingly close to blowing this gig altogether, and with it the opportunity for a staff job at Galloway and Donnelly. Which would leave me back where I started. Unsure of my next paycheck, no insurance, no security. The whole point was to shift things so that in the long run I could do what satisfied me creatively and still be a financially responsible human. So I'm trying again.

Anyhow, as I was saying about bliss. Turns out Daniel is secretly talented, and not just in the boudoir. He's got these designs for the most imaginative and wonderful buildings. What's even cooler is that he showed them to me, and he says I'm the first person ever to see them!!!

The longer I know him the more I like him. But I think, and this is just conjecture here, that when he's with me the real Daniel comes out to play. He stifles himself for his boring work and his boring family. With me, it's the real deal. Like his drawings. It's a very heady feeling, and one I fear that lends itself to assigning it more weight than I should.

Why is it women go straight to love, not passing Go, not collecting two hundred dollars? I'm serious here. I swore I wasn't going to go there with Daniel. I did it with Gordon and ended up in emotional intensive care. So why, when he looks at me with his sweet blue eyes, and his smile is slow and teasing, do I think he loves me? That he wants to get married, convert, have three kids, build me a house in the country. Instead of, wow, this is very cool. We're into each other today, how lucky is that?

Can someone explain this? Please???

Uh-oh, I have a hysterical director screaming out my name. I'll write again later.

Bye

M

INCREDIBLY GRATEFUL it was the weekend, Daniel leaned on the wall of the elevator going up to his apartment. It should have been a good week. Since they'd gotten the go-ahead on the Bressler project, he'd been in meetings with the clients going over details, which was a long and exhausting process. In the past he'd enjoyed this part, because he was one of those that believed that God was in the details. But these jerks had no imagination. Traditional was fine, but they put the kibosh on anything that had even a hint of creativity.

It didn't matter. He was home now, and looking forward to spending time with Margot. The hours had gotten the better of her the last few days, and they'd spent the nights apart. He'd missed her, but he'd appreciated getting some much needed rest.

It had surprised him how many times he'd thought of her. He'd called her at least once a day but usually twice. Last night, even though she'd said she was dead on her feet, he'd gone to her place, and it was only guilt that made him turn around before knocking on the door.

He walked down the hall, thinking about getting in the shower, and stopped short when he saw the red envelope taped to his door. Printed in block letters was "Open Me."

He did, and found a note. "Daniel…shower, relax, dress pretty. Expect to be kidnapped at nine. Oh, and eat something light, too." It was signed with an extravagant M.

Kidnapped? Sounded good to him. He went inside and got himself a beer before stripping off his work clothes. He wasn't the least bit sure of how to dress "pretty," but he figured she meant in the new clothes. But first, shower. A long one, to get out all the kinks.

He smiled. Maybe not all the kinks.

MARGOT CHECKED HERSELF one last time in the full-length mirror behind her bedroom door. Her hair was down, the way Daniel liked it, but swept at the side with a glittery pin. She'd worn darker, more dramatic makeup which seemed right, considering where they were going. She giggled, thinking about it. Daniel was going to *plotz!* She couldn't wait to see his expression. One thing was guaranteed, though. They were going to both get lucky tonight. Real lucky.

Back to the assessment. Her shirt was red, tightish and very low cut. In fact, she'd had to wear her demi-bra, which made her knockers look huge. No necklace, no dangly earrings. Cleavage was the statement.

Her skirt was black, and made her butt look good, so yay. Black heels that didn't even hurt and she was a hap-penin' babe.

She knew just what she wanted Daniel to wear, and her first note to him had been specific, but then she'd thrown that one out. She could rearrange him when she got there.

It was just past nine. Time to skedaddle.

She got her bag, which had only enough room for breath mints, key, lip gloss and some cash. It was warm enough out that she didn't need a jacket, and it would be very warm where they were going.

One last thing. In her bathroom, she took out her fa-vorite perfume, Samsara, sprayed it in front of herself and walked into the mist. Perfection.

She went to Daniel's, her heart beating a little faster with each step. After her miserable week, this was just the treat she needed. Cool music, Daniel and lots of nasty. Could it get any better?

She knocked twice, and the door flew open. Daniel met her with a smile that would have made even a pro-fessional grump get happy.

The kiss was even better. Cool lips, hot tongue, thrust and parry…everything kissing should be plus he tasted like Heineken and toothpaste, which they should market immediately.

"You're gorgeous," he said as he stood back and scoped her out. "Good choice on the shirt."

She grinned. "Merci." The she took a tour around him. He was close to just right. Very close. The shirt he had on was très retro—gray, with white piping, smooth lines and a faboo triangular pocket. The jeans were faded and tight fitting, making his ass look like something from the Louvre. The problem came with footwear. She felt sure they'd let him in, but eyebrows would arch over the loafers. "Shoes."

He did his blinky thing. "Shoes?"

"May I see yours?"

He looked down at his feet, clearly not understanding.

"I mean the ones you're not currently wearing."

"Oh. Uh, sure." He led her to his bedroom, and opened his closet.

Adorable how he'd put all his new clothes on one side, as if they'd contaminate his Republican uniforms. But she wasn't here for a critique. She found his shoes in very neat order on a rack that ran along the bottom of the closet.

Nothing, horrible, eh, maybe, horrible, horrible, no way in hell, maybe and horrible. Okay, there were two maybe's and the only one that would work for his current outfit were the wing tips. She bent, making sure he was watching from the appropriate vantage point, and got the shoes. Which she handed to him.

Daniel opened his mouth as if to question, then closed it again, went to his bed, sat and switched shoes. Then he stood up to give her the total view.

"Excellent."

"I'm so pleased you approve."

She held out her arm, crooked at the elbow. "Shall we away?"

"I'll call for the carriage."

"Oohh, interesting. But too far out of our way. Taxi."

"Taxi it is."

"Are you going to tell me where we're going?"

Margot shook her head. "You'll find out."

"Do I need anything special?"

"Not a thing. Just a sense of adventure."

He grinned. "You're on."

DANIEL HAD NO IDEA where they were. Greenwich Village, but he'd never been in this particular area, and never at night. It was dark. Not just because it was night, but because they were still in the city, and there were virtually no lights. Streetlights, yes, but they seemed really dim. And either the shopkeepers had all decided to close their curtains all at once, or there was nothing behind the dark glass of the buildings. Except Margot told the cabdriver to pull up in front of one of the dark shops.

He paid the man, then held the door for her, liking that she took his extended hand and smiled up into his face as she stepped onto the sidewalk.

"Come," she said, keeping hold of his hand. "This way."

"Are you sure this is where we're supposed to be?"

Her laugh said yep, and he followed her to a staircase leading down. He was worried, her in her heels, that she couldn't see, but she didn't hesitate at all. Just walked as if she'd been there often.

A door at the bottom, no sign, just a knob. She opened it slowly, as if she were leading him into a haunted house, which for all he knew, she might be. And finally, a light. Neon. Red. Above yet another door, but this one had a curtain.

She squeezed his hand, and he wondered if she could tell his pulse wasn't in the least steady, and that if it wasn't for this particular woman, he'd never be here, and it wouldn't bother him to have missed it.

Then they were behind the curtain. It was still dark, but he could make out a woman with dark hair, dark makeup, dark clothes, pale skin sitting behind a desk. A silver ring glittered in her nose.

Margot walked them up to the table, and handed the woman some money. He wasn't able to see how much.

"Let me," he said, whispering, although he wasn't sure why.

"My treat."

"Hey—"

A finger touched his lips. "My treat. Now come on."

And again she led him to yet another curtained doorway. Only this time, she slipped her arm around his waist, and he wasn't quite certain if it was to be close or to prevent him from bolting.

Inside, there was a little more light, although not much. A dark carpeted hallway led them to a sharp right turn. She walked faster as they entered a small room. There, on the wall, was a painting of a woman.

It was an art gallery. Of course. But not like any he'd seen before. This painting… He'd stopped in front of it, his brain not quite registering what was in front of him.

She was naked. In restraints. Her hair was deep auburn, long, flowing. Her face was beautiful although he couldn't see her eyes because they were closed. She seemed to be in ecstasy. The bindings, thick rope, around her wrists and her ankles, were incredibly erotic. If he'd had to guess at the name of the piece, he would have gone with *The Orgasm*.

Margot moved closer to him and he jumped at the contact. His gaze went from the painting to the woman pressing against his side, and there was a new image in his mind's eye. Margot, naked, bound. His.

"You like?" she asked.

He nodded. "You have a keen eye for art."

"Well, I remembered that you liked…stuff. And I thought this might be your kind of, well, stuff."

He leaned over and kissed her, invading her mouth with the urgency that had taken over his body. She sucked on his tongue, making him moan, and he pulled her tighter against him.

She ran her hand down his side, then snuck it in between them, lowering it to cover the bulge in his pants. He hissed at the touch, and bucked into her palm.

"There's more," she said, pulling away, leaving him aching.

"I don't know if I can take more."

"Sure you can." She grabbed him by the middle of his belt and dragged him to the next cubicle.

He was almost afraid to look at the painting. But he

turned his head anyway. This one was a different woman, a rounder woman, also naked. She stood next to a large bed with red satin sheets. Her head was bowed and her hands were handcuffed behind her back. There was a tattoo on her hip, a bloodred rose. Behind her on the wall there was a shadow of a man. Actually, more the suggestion of a man. But Daniel's gaze went back to the woman. Blond, her hair pulled up on the back of her head, much the same way that Margot wore hers. The woman in the painting was looking down in a sub-missive gesture, but her shoulders were back, her breasts, round and heavy, jutted proudly. The soft curve of her belly drew him in, and then he couldn't help but trace her plump behind.

"Tell me what you're thinking," Margot whispered, her warm breath touching his neck.

"That she reminds me of you."

"Really?"

"In a very good way."

"Thank you."

He ran his hand down the center of her back. "You'd look beautiful like that."

"With a tattoo?"

"In handcuffs."

"I see."

He looked at her, wishing the light was better so he could read her eyes. "I can see I'd better be careful what I tell you."

"Why?"

"Because if you know too much, you could use it against me."

"Would you mind?"

He shook his head.

Her smile was wicked, and grew more so as she brought up her hand and crooked her finger to make him bend closer. "I have another surprise."

"Oh, God."

"But I'm not going to tell you till we get to the end of the exhibit."

He stood straighter. "You're a cruel, cruel woman."

"I know," she said, clearly delighted with her diabolical self.

"Well, come on. Let's see the rest."

"There's wine first," she said.

"No."

"Yes. Follow, please."

"Cruel, I tell you."

Laughing, she led him down a short hall. When he got to the next room, he was surprised to find others were already there. He'd assumed... Of course there'd be other people. Art gallery. Duh. Most of them looked normal, but there were a few that were decked out in leather and skin. Mostly skin. Nothing that would land them in jail, but close.

One woman, who had to be at least six-two, wore a tight bustier that didn't quite cover her nipples. And what was basically a thong in the back so her butt was bare. She had on some black nylons, but there wasn't much left to the imagination. Then she turned and he saw there was a zipper over her crotch.

Margot tugged him down. "The better to eat you with, my dear," she whispered.

His face got hot, and the bulge in his pants became more pronounced. He decided to get some wine, drink it quickly and get on with the tour.

With Margot beside him, he picked up two plastic glasses of white wine, Daniel polishing his off in two gulps. Margot, damn her, sipped, eyeing the crowd.

The artist, a woman, stood by her portrait. She was the most normal looking of the bunch. In her forties, plump, wearing a plain black dress, she looked as if she could be the president of the PTA, not busy painting naked women in chains.

"How did you find out about this?"

"Devon. He knows the gallery owner."

"Are all the exhibits like this?"

"Mostly. Controversial, for sure, but not always B and D."

"So you've been here before."

"Oh, yeah. Devon sometimes models."

"Really?"

"Naked and everything."

"Eric doesn't mind?"

"No." She turned her head slightly to the left and ran her pink tongue over her juicy lower lip. "Would you?"

"I don't care what Devon does."

She smiled. "Cute. If someone you loved were to get naked for a painting."

He didn't have to think. "Oh, yeah."

"Really?"

"I take it you wouldn't."

"I think you should be immortalized. But it should be sculpture, not paint."

"You know just what to say to render me speechless."

"It's a gift."

"Tell you what another gift would be."

"What's that?"

"Getting out of here."

"But we haven't seen it all."

"There's only one woman I want to see naked, and she's not on any of these walls."

Margot blushed fetchingly. "My, my, Daniel. You are a sweet-talking devil."

"I try."

"Okay. Let's go home."

"Yippee."

"Careful, I'm beginning to think you didn't like my surprise."

"Like it? My happiness is growing exponentially. Which is why we need to leave soon before I embarrass both of us."

She put her hand back on his fly, not even trying for discretion. "You could never embarrass me with this. Choke me, yes. Embarrass, no."

He snatched her hand and went back the way they'd come.

"Hey!"

He stopped abruptly in the next room in front of the painting of the blonde and the handcuffs. Looked into Margot's eyes, the dark depths shadowed by her long lashes. "That was very naughty, Margot."

Her mouth opened in a small gasp. "I suppose it was."

"I'm afraid I can't just let that go."

She didn't say anything, just nodded, her breathing getting faster, shallower.

He bent down to kiss her, but segued to her lower lip, which he took between his teeth. He bit her just hard enough to hear that gasp once more. "I suggest," he whispered, "you try to be very good all the way home."

"I'll try, but it won't be easy."

"No?"

She shook her head slowly. "I haven't told you my secret."

He arched his eyebrow, waiting, trying like hell to keep his expression stern.

She took a step back and put her hands flat on her skirt. Then she slowly lifted her hem, inching the material up her thighs. He was physically incapable of breathing as she continued the ascent until finally, he could see the exact nature of her secret.

13

MARGOT FOUGHT NOT TO SQUIRM as she revealed herself to Daniel. Not only had she gone commando, but yesterday she'd stolen an hour and had gotten a Brazilian wax, which right this second felt completely worth the pain.

He stared at her with such hunger that heat unfurled like a dozen ribbons in her belly. She'd known the pictures in the gallery would excite him. The memory of him holding her arms above her head in her bed was still vivid in her mind. Although she hadn't asked him, she was pretty darn sure he'd never played the kind of games she had in mind for tonight. To live out his fantasy, to hold her captive and at his whim. She just hoped that in the years since his first fantasy he'd gotten a lot more specific about his desires.

Of course, she had a few of her own. She hadn't done much in the way of bondage games, but what she'd tried, she'd liked. And she'd never been with someone who stirred up more intense feelings. When he touched her…

Daniel cleared his throat, his gaze still riveted to the juncture of her thighs. "We'd better go, or they're going to get a completely different kind of show right here."

She released her skirt. Daniel touched the side of her

cheek with the palm of his hand, looking at her with wonder and desire. Margot sighed as she closed her eyes.

His hand moved slowly through her hair until he was at the back of her head. His grip slowly tightened, not hurting her, but in control.

She opened her eyes as he tugged her head back. The desire of seconds ago had turned to flames and he took her mouth, kissing her long and deep. Slow smoldering gave way to sizzling, the undercurrent of danger making her squeeze her legs together.

Greedy lips slanted and grasped hers. Heated breath mingled, and she moaned as he pulled her body close. She strained against him, wanting much more than was possible, at least for now.

Daniel's mouth moved to her neck to nip, then soothe. Still captive in his arms she could only touch his sides, too little of his back. Yet the caress made him moan, spurred him to take her lips once more, brutally. When he finally pulled back, it was just an inch. She felt his hot breath as he whispered, "Let's get out of here."

With an unsteady gait, she followed him through the brief maze of rooms back onto the street. There were no cabs in sight, and they walked east until they found a more crowded street. They didn't speak, but they touched, hands at first, then Daniel slipped his arm around her waist, and she returned the favor, so their bodies skimmed together with each step.

She felt high, as if she'd had too much champagne, but it was just knowing what was to come. Anticipation was her drug, and the search for a free taxi seemed to last forever.

Finally, Daniel waved down a cab. He opened the door for her and she kept a completely straight face as she crawled in, purposely letting her skirt ride up to the point of indecency.

He groaned as he joined her, his voice a low growl telling the driver their address.

Once they started moving, Daniel moved his hand to her thigh. Keeping his face forward, not even glancing her way, he slipped his fingers between her thighs, almost touching her newly smooth mons, but not quite.

Wanting more, she spread her knees, but he kept up the teasing, brushing her flesh with the very tips of his fingers, so lightly it was almost a tickle. She scooted forward, trying to get him to move up, but all she got for her trouble was stillness. He didn't move at all.

When she shifted back into her original position, he started petting her again. She smiled, liking this. Liking it a lot.

Tonight would be new for both of them, and she wanted to see him strip off his politeness, bare down to the animal that lurked inside the architect.

So she sat quite motionless as he teased her, wanting more pressure, willing his fingers to move up, letting the frustration and ache build as they drove through the New York night.

By the time they reached their building, she was wet and hot and ravenous for the man paying the driver. No elevator could be fast enough for her, especially not this one, but Daniel had other ideas. He led her away from the staircase to the elevator and he pressed the button.

When she looked at him, he was all stern and forceful, his eyes brilliant with power, and she doubted she'd ever been this turned on in her life.

He didn't touch her, but he held her quite immobile just the same. She didn't dare move or speak for fear he'd stop the game again.

When the elevator opened, he nodded for her to enter first. He joined her, turned to face the front. With agonizing slowness, the doors hissed shut. Then Daniel spun to face her. "Lift your skirt," he said.

Her cheeks burned and her mouth felt dry as she obeyed. Moving slowly, she spread her legs a bit, then for the second time that night she inched the black material up her thighs. Cool air hit her sensitive flesh, caressed her moist nether lips.

Daniel's eyes glittered with intensity as he took her in from face to thigh and back again. He wet his lower lip, but he still didn't make a move.

The elevator made its slow ascent to the third floor as she felt more and more naked and needy. Her body yearned for his touch, for release.

Just as they slowed to a stop, Daniel closed the distance between them. He reached down and brushed his finger inside her. She trembled at the contact, missing him the second he pulled away.

He smiled in a way that gave her goose bumps as the door behind him opened.

She released her skirt, then walked with him to her door, his hand on the small of her back. It took her two tries to fit the key in the lock.

Once inside, Daniel led her straight to the bedroom.

He turned on the light, the one with the red scarf, and the room became a warm rose-colored cave.

He sat on the edge of her bed and slipped off his shoes. The smile came back as he got comfortable against her pillows. "Take off your clothes," he said, his voice little more than a hoarse, smoky whisper.

She gripped her shirt and pulled it slowly up over her head, and dropped it at her feet. Then she reached back to unclasp her bra, but he shook his head.

"Leave it on."

Her hands went to the zipper of her skirt, which she pulled down with shaking fingers. The skirt pooled around her ankles. She felt more naked in the demibra than she would have if she'd been completely undressed. It felt delicious and wanton, and just seeing the lust in his eyes made her feel exquisite.

He watched her as he got out of his own clothes, baring that incredible chest, his small dusky nipples hard and pointed. He stood, never shifting his gaze, and undid his pants. He pushed them off along with his briefs, and kicked them out of the way.

She'd known he was hard back at the gallery, but seeing him huge, hot and straining made her giddy with her own power.

She moved toward him slowly until she was close enough to feel his heat. Unable to resist, she ran her fingertips down the center of his chest, letting the silky dark hair slow her descent. When she reached his belly button she lingered, slipping her pinky into the tiny indent.

He sucked in a harsh breath, put his hands on her shoulders. His lips on her ear, he nibbled on the lobe, then licked a shivery circle around the shell. "Lie down," he whispered, the moist heat of his breath making her crazy.

She climbed on the bed, on her back, and waited. He would tell her what to do next, and whatever it was, she would obey eagerly. As long as he didn't make her wait too long.

Daniel took his time as he savored the beauty lying before him. She was everything a woman should be: soft, round, pale and so incredibly hot. That she'd taken him to see the gallery, that she'd bared herself right there, where anyone could have walked in on them, and then again on the elevator. It was more than his brain could take. Of course, there wasn't very much blood up there, since it was all pooled elsewhere. What was left was more basic and feral than anything he'd ever experienced. He felt like a caveman, a brute, and yet there was this overwhelming need to still be in control, to design this experience so that it was as exciting for her as it was for him.

Even though he was more than ready to climb on top of her, he wasn't going to rush through this. Making her wait was crucial to his plan. He wanted her to burst into flames, to scream his name when he finally let her come.

He leaned over her, taking in the enticing details of her face, the way her eyes glittered even though they were half closed, the shimmer of her lips, the hint of white teeth. "I'm going to tie you up," he said, making sure his voice was even and almost cold. "I want you ready."

Her mouth opened wider as she inhaled, her chest

rose letting her pink nipples show, making her little ring glitter, but only for a moment.

He straightened, watching as her hands eased up over her white comforter, then shyly inched their way out, until they were reaching for the top of the four-poster. Then her legs moved, stretching, until they, too, were ready for binding.

He ran his gaze up those long legs, right to where she was unbearably naked. Forcing himself to move on, he went to her closet, where he knew she hung her scarves. He selected four of the longest, running the material over his own thigh to make sure they were soft enough for her delicate limbs.

When he turned back, she was still in position. He didn't think it was possible, but he got harder. In fact, he had to look away, think of last year's basketball finals, while he calmed the hell down.

When he could think straight again, he ran one of the scarves down her right leg, loving the tremble he caused. He took her slim ankle in his hand, bent low and kissed the arch of her foot, and she moaned softly.

He wrapped her ankle twice, using the blue-and-white scarf, then pulled her tighter before fastening her to the sturdy wood of her bedpost.

Knowing he wasn't going to last if he kept this up, he moved more quickly to her left leg, but he couldn't resist. He lifted this foot to his mouth, and slipped her big toe in his mouth.

That got an even more dramatic reaction. Her hips lifted and her eyes fluttered. He used the yellow scarf, shifting her body as he tugged her into place.

Then it was her left wrist. This he kissed on the soft, thin skin on the inside before he made sure she was spread out like a butterfly.

He walked around the bed, drinking her as he skimmed her thigh, her calf, the curve of her hip. And then he used the last scarf and she was his. To do with as he pleased. To tease, torment, pleasure until she begged him to stop.

"Oh, God," she whispered, her voice fluttery and high. "Please."

He sat down next to her. Touched the satiny skin under her bra. Delighted that with her pulled so taut those hard little nipples were just visible. Available. Irresistible.

He leaned over her and licked the tender bud, swirled his tongue around and around. Her body arched as much as it could, pushing her into his hungry mouth.

He sucked her in, gently at first, then harder, pulling her until she cried out, and then he was gentle again, swirling and licking, feeling the edge of her bra under his lower lip.

She squirmed beneath him, moving that delectable rump back and forth, her hands opening and closing in rapid spasms. Her head back, her throat exposed and vulnerable. And her hair, oh, her hair was luxurious and vibrant and he wanted to spend a week rolling in it, but not right now. Now, he had a duty to a neglected nipple.

He shifted over her body, taking the point between his teeth. She shivered as he increased the pressure, careful not to hurt her…too much.

Her low groan told him he'd given her just what she wanted. His head spun as he sucked her deeply, as if he was somewhere outside himself, watching as the banquet of this woman lay spread before him. It was his fantasies come to life, and the odd thing was, the most important part was taking Margot further and deeper than she'd ever dreamed of going.

His hands moved over her sides and her stomach, as always astonished at the softness of her. There were no sharp angles, nothing jarring. Only smooth, hot velvet.

"Daniel…"

He looked up, pained to part with her taste.

"More," she said, her head lifted off the pillow, her gaze filled with need.

"I say what happens now," he said.

She whimpered and the sound went right to his balls.

"And I say you get more." He moved up until he could capture her in a kiss.

MARGOT COULDN'T BREATHE. Stretched to the limit, every muscle in her body begging for relief, her hands grasping uselessly, desperately needing something to hang on to. And his relentless tongue kept up the exquisite torture.

He'd made her come twice tonight, and she couldn't believe she was at the brink of yet another orgasm. Her eyes closed tightly, she focused as her body revved up to the crescendo. She felt his body between her legs, his sweaty knees between her own. Bent over her as if drinking from a stream, he was anything but mild. Possessed was more like it. Determined to kill her with the pointy end of his tongue, with his long, thick fingers.

There it was…almost, almost…

She cried out as the spasm started, as her stomach

contracted and the lights exploded behind her eyes. Bucking and writhing, dying to be free of the ropes even as she thrilled at her captivity, she was reduced to nothing but sensation as wave after wave carried her to where time stopped.

Calming down took a while, helped by Daniel's gentle hands caressing her thighs as he sat up. When she opened her eyes, he was looking at her, a very satisfied expression on his incredible face.

"Beautiful," he said with that smoky voice.

"I feel like I was rode hard and put away wet."

He laughed, and that sound, too, had the rough edges of desire.

Margot's gaze slipped down his chest to where he was slowly stroking himself. "I think it's your turn."

"Me, too," he said. "But there's something I have to do first."

He couldn't possibly expect her to come again. Her head flopped back on the pillow, trying to slow her rapid heart. She'd had sex before, oh yeah, even with Daniel, but this? This needed a completely different word. Something with a large number of vowels.

He climbed off the bed and she shivered as she remembered his talented tongue in so many unexpected places. By the time he'd gotten to the main course, she'd been ready to pop at a stiff breeze. And he'd given her much, much more than that.

Surprised, she turned to watch as he untied her left wrist. "Oh."

He rubbed her flesh where the scarf had been, eliciting many tingles. "Is something wrong?"

"No, not at all. I just figured…"

"That I'd want you tied for more stuff?"

She nodded.

"I thought about it," he said as he walked around the bed to get to the other wrist. "But I want your hands available for this next part."

"I can deal with that."

He smiled at her, but frankly she didn't spare his grin much attention. She was too busy looking at his erection. Which had flagged, but not by much. The man had been hard forever. She didn't know how he could stand it. "I'm impressed," she said.

"Thank you."

"I would have expected you to be, well, a little more impatient."

He looked at her with puzzled eyes, and then something clicked. "You didn't know?"

"What?"

"I'm on round two."

She brought her free hands together and rubbed them. "Really? Where was I?"

"Screaming my name."

"Ah."

"It was quite effective."

"I could have sworn you never stopped touching me."

"I didn't."

"Then how?"

"Spontaneous combustion."

She blinked. "Wow."

"Wow, indeed. But this time, I think I'd like more participation."

She nodded, anxious now that he finish with the scarves. He seemed a little anxious himself by the time he got to the last one.

When she was free, he lay beside her and for a long moment, he simply looked into her eyes. She was the one, finally, to roll over and grab the condom, wishing she didn't have to bother. After ripping it open, she sat up, a little dizzy after all that blood rushing south, and went to put it on him. But first, she decided he deserved a little quid pro quo.

She breathed in the essence of Daniel before she tasted him. Salty and pungent, it was the taste of sex itself. Running her tongue carefully over the entire length of him, she then licked her own hand, lubricating the palm that grasped him at the base.

His groan shook the bed as she took him inside her mouth. His hips were already rocking restlessly, and he had lapsed into wordless sounds, tiny moans and whimpers that turned into long growled protest when she pulled away. But she didn't keep him stranded for long.

Her lips returned, and she tasted more of him, her hand gliding up and down the veined shaft.

He groaned when she pointed her tongue and rubbed him where he liked it best, but then she was knocked back when he sat up in a fury. He took her by the shoulders and pushed her to her back.

Despite her best intentions, he ended up fitting the condom on himself with shaking fingers, and then he was over her, straining on straightened arms, his face inches from her own. His hot breath warmed her as he leaned down to take possession of her lips.

His knees positioned her and his hard length went right where it was supposed to, and when his tongue thrust deeply into her mouth, his cock thrust lower.

She cried out against his lips, curled her legs around his hips and hung on for all she was worth. Nothing gentle here, just a man out of control, giving her everything, all of him. And she taking it and wanting more.

His neck arched and his jaw clenched, and she could trace the lines of his muscles as he thrust into her, long strokes, so hard, so hot. She dug her nails into his back as her own pleasure made her insides tremble. Daniel's thrusts got faster, shorter, and she watched his face transform into the mask of pleasure-pain that was the instant before orgasm. One last time he ground into her with his whole body driving him, and he cried out from somewhere deep and primal as he surrendered.

LATER, WHEN SLEEP WAS seconds away, he made one last effort. He leaned over to the woman curled around him, her face ghostly pale with only the light of the moon, her eyes closed, her lips slightly parted. He kissed her. "Thank you," he whispered.

He rested his head back on the pillow, still not quite understanding what had happened to him. Who he was. All he knew for sure was that he liked this guy.

14

HER DOORBELL WOKE HER, and Margot sat up in bed, positive she'd only been asleep for ten minutes. But the sun came through the windows brightly, not just an early-morning peek.

Daniel was still asleep, his head sideways on the pillow, quiet and peaceful and achingly handsome.

Another knock spurred her to get up. Her bedside clock told her it was just past ten, so it could be anyone, but probably it was Corrie.

Margot grabbed her robe and hurried to the front door to find she'd been right. Her neighbor, looking sad and angry, gazed at her with pleading eyes.

"I'll give you my life savings if you'll make coffee while I go pee," she said. "Then we can talk, okay?"

Corrie nodded, giving her the first smile she'd seen from the woman in days.

Margot couldn't wait, though. She dashed back to the bedroom, grabbed some clothes, then closed herself in the bathroom. By the time she came back to the kitchen the scent of coffee filled the room and Corrie, bless her heart, had already prepared her a mug exactly how she liked it.

She sat down across from her friend and looked into her haunted eyes. "Talk to me."

Corrie tried, but she didn't say anything for a long while. She dabbed at tears, stopping them before they could escape down her cheeks. Finally, after she blew her nose, she stood up, poured herself coffee and came back to the table. "It isn't going to work," she said, her voice soft and beaten. "I get it now. There's just nothing I can do. He wants something else. I'm not even sure what, just not me. Not me."

"Has he told you what he does want?"

"Not in so many words. But everything I do is wrong. My cooking sucks, the house is never clean enough, I don't have a job, I don't read enough, I'm not smart enough. Me. It's me he can't stand."

"What are you going to do?"

"That's the thing. I don't know. You don't happen to have ten grand sitting around, do you? That would really help."

"Is it all about money?"

"Let's just say money would make this a lot easier. I'd be thrilled with a job, too."

"I don't have much of a savings account, but you're welcome to it."

Corrie's mouth quirked up at the corners. "So that offer you made me this morning wasn't worth much, huh?"

"Nope. But I'm still grateful for the coffee."

Corrie sniffed again. "The only thing I can do is go back to dancing. And I'm so damn out of shape, I can't even… Oh, God, I never thought I'd have to do that again."

"There has to be something else you can do. Maybe there's something at the advertising agency."

"That would be great," Corrie said, her hopes clearly not very high.

"I'll do what I can."

Corrie stared at her hands, unblinking, while Margot went through different scenarios. It wasn't likely that she could get Corrie work, but there was a chance. She'd check it out first thing Monday. In the meantime, she wanted to keep her friend busy. Too much alone time now wasn't wise. She'd call the boys, get them to pitch in, which they would, because they loved Corrie, too.

Nels had been acting like a prick to Corrie for way too long. But Corrie loved him with all her heart. And what mattered was that Corrie get through this with the least amount of damage.

"I don't get it," Corrie said. "I've tried so hard."

"You shouldn't have to change to make anyone happy," Margot said, her anger rising, making her want to go up to his apartment and slap the bastard around for a few days. "No one should expect you to."

"That's funny, coming from you."

"What does that mean?"

"Come on, Margot. All you do is change people. Look at Daniel. Look at how he's dressing now, his hair. Hell, his whole attitude. You're building him into the guy you want him to be."

"I am not."

"Look, I'm not accusing you, Margot, I'm just telling it the way it is. But it's okay, because Daniel doesn't seem to mind."

Sitting back in her chair, Margot reached for her coffee, but didn't pick it up. "I don't think this is the same thing, Corrie. What I'm doing with Daniel is just for, you know, fun."

"Is it?"

"It's just clothes, and you have to admit, his were awful."

"Agreed. But is it right? You hate Nels for the very same thing. He wants me to be someone I'm not. You want Daniel to be Gordon."

"No, that's not true. Maybe the changing him part is, but not into Gordon. I've worked too hard on all the ways Gordon was wrong for me. Daniel's nothing like him."

"But he sure dresses like him."

Margot felt her throat constrict and her heart slam in her chest. "Corrie, please."

Her friend reached across the table and touched her hand. "I'm not trying to hurt you, sweetie. You're the most wonderful human I know. I just can't tell any more lies. Not to Nels, not to you, not to myself. I can't."

"Lies? You really believe I'm lying to myself?"

Corrie sighed. "I don't know. Listen, I'm sorry. I'm a wreck and an idiot. Ignore everything I said."

"Like that's possible." Margot got up, walked over to the kitchen sink, but there weren't any dirty dishes in it to wash, so she just ran the sponge over the clean counter.

"Shit," Corrie said behind her. "Just call me Little Mary Sunshine. Bringing a little joy into everyone's life."

"It's okay, Corrie. You've just given me something to think about. Doesn't mean I'm taking your word as gospel."

"Hallelujah, sister."

"Hey, Corrie, how's it going?" Daniel asked, trying to stifle a yawn.

Margot spun around, as did Corrie, to find Daniel, his hair a wild mess, a sleep line cutting across his chin, and he still was such a knockout it made Margot's heart kick into high gear. It didn't hurt that all he had on were his jeans. No shirt. No shoes. How come men with no shoes looked so sexy?

As he walked toward Margot, he put his hand on Corrie's shoulder and kissed her on the cheek, oh, so sweetly.

"Everything's peachy, Daniel," Corrie said. "Thanks for asking."

Daniel pulled back and raised his eyebrows at Margot, who could only offer him a shrug in return. He got himself a cup of coffee then sat down next to Corrie. After he took a sip, he leaned forward. "I don't know your husband," he said, "but I think I've gotten to know you. And the people who care about you. If Nels can't see what a great woman you are, then it's his loss. Which doesn't make any of this easier, but hey, I'm just saying it like I see it. If there's anything I can do…"

Corrie smiled. "Thanks. You don't happen to know of a job for someone who can't do much, do you?"

"Not offhand, but I'll ask around."

Corrie finished her coffee, then stood up. "I've got class in half an hour, and I'm not ready," she said. "But I'll call later."

Margot gave her a hug. "We'll have dinner tonight, okay?"

"Great. See you guys later." She got to the door, and turned back to face the kitchen. "Oh, and, Daniel—swell hickies."

Margot looked at Daniel, and saw exactly what Corrie meant. She didn't remember doing that to him, but clearly, she'd been a busy girl. Not only was he marked on his chest, three times, his neck looked as if he'd been hit with the pox.

He wasn't looking too thrilled about it, either. "Tell me it's only on my chest."

Wincing, Margot shook her head.

"My shirt'll cover it, right?"

She shook her head again. "You have any turtlenecks?"

He let his head drop onto his hand. "Great. They're already suspicious at the office."

Margot joined him at the table. "What do you mean?"

"Nothing. Just, the haircut, and those clothes I wore."

"You're kidding? They can't get on you for looking good."

"It's not a question of good. It's a question of what's appropriate. But those things aren't really the issue."

"What is?"

"Well, damn it, I'm supposed to be working on another project, an office building for a CPA."

"That's good, isn't it?"

"It would be, but all they want is the same crap I just finished. They don't want to hear any new ideas, nothing original."

"Haven't you been doing that kind of design for a while now?"

He nodded. "That's the problem."

"But you love your job."

"I love architecture. I'd like to do something different every once in a while, you know? Something that doesn't look like it was built a hundred years ago."

Margot sipped her drink, even though it wasn't very warm anymore. She thought about what Corrie had said, and hoped like hell that Daniel's dissatisfaction with his work didn't have anything to do with her.

"Hey."

She looked up to meet Daniel's gaze, which sent shivers of wonderfulness all through her. "Hey, back atya."

"Last night…"

She waggled her eyebrows.

"You can say that again."

She touched the back of his hand. "You were astounding."

"Yeah, I kinda was," he said, grinning adorably. "But look who I had for a teacher."

"Pish tosh. As you recall, I didn't do much more than lie there, looking naked."

He turned his hand over and squeezed hers. "I was thinking a shower might be in order. But there's this place on my back that I just can't reach."

She widened her eyes innocently. "I have a long loofah you can borrow."

"Yeah, I've got your long loofah right here, baby."

She cracked up, loving it when Daniel got silly. Which he did more and more. He might be changing, but the new Daniel was really just the relaxed, comfy Daniel. Nothing wrong with that.

He stood up, still holding on to her hand, and led her

through the house. By the time they reached the bedroom, her robe was on the floor, his jeans were undone and showering would have to wait.

THE THIRD TIME they were in charge of the main course, it was Daniel's turn to cook. He checked the game hens in the oven, per Margot's instructions, although he wasn't totally sure what he was looking for. They appeared to be browning, and there was a certain amount of sizzle happening, which was about all you could ask of dead fowl. He closed the oven and glanced around the kitchen. Oddly, they'd never ventured to his place, but he didn't mind. He liked cooking with Margot. He liked doing a lot of things with Margot.

What he hadn't realized was how much time he'd spent with her over the last couple of months. The fact had come home to him yesterday when he'd gotten a call from Terry. His buddy had subtly inquired if he'd recently been returned to Earth by the aliens who'd kidnapped him, because certainly if he'd been around, he would have called his friends, perhaps even wanted to get together.

Thoroughly chastised, Daniel had explained about Margot, and Terry had been his usual supportive self by telling him to start thinking with something other than his dick.

That's why Terry and Bill were coming to the tenant's dinner tonight, despite the fact that they weren't tenants.

Margot had approved, however, and she seemed to be looking forward to meeting his friends. It was time.

Time for him to bring some of his old world into the new. Of course, he hadn't told his family about Margot. No need. Besides, his conversations with his mother didn't usually include more than a few words about his life. But he sure as hell knew what she was doing with her week.

He tried to imagine their reaction to Margot. She was so far away from anyone he'd ever gone out with. Her clothes, her style, her background. Everything about her was what his parents regarded as suspect, "other" and that was not acceptable. Not at all. But there was something perversely appealing in the idea of bringing her to a Sunday supper. Just to see the constipated look on his father's face, to see what his mother would offer up as dinner conversation. It would be an experience.

"Are you almost ready?"

He looked up to see Margot walking through the living room. She looked incredible in a long, slinky black dress and red sandals that matched her lips. She'd left her hair down, but there was a brilliant red flower behind her right ear.

He wanted her.

He always wanted her. When he wasn't with her, he thought about her. When he was with her he wanted to be closer. Everything fell together when they were in bed. Not just having sex, although God knows, that was his favorite activity, but reading, or just being close. He loved watching her sleep, even when she snored. She was adamant that she never did. Not all the time, and not like a foghorn or anything. He liked it. He liked her.

As she smiled, it hit him how much. The idea of not

being with Margot wasn't something he wanted to explore. This was the best time he'd ever had, and he wanted it to go on for the foreseeable future. Learning all about Margot was a long-term process, and he was in for as long as she'd have him.

She entered the kitchen and gave him a quick kiss before she looked around at the dinner preparations. Everything was ready. Dishes, glasses, silver, napkins. The rice pilaf was cooked, and the others were bringing the rest of the meal.

Appetizers were at Devon and Eric's tonight, and they were due there in about ten minutes, which meant that Bill and Terry should have been here by now.

"What's wrong?"

He hadn't realized Margot was looking at him. "The guys aren't here yet."

"Parking's a bitch. I'm sure they're trying to find a space right now."

"Yeah, you're probably—"

A knock on the door ended that little discussion, and Daniel felt a surprising tension in his gut. He wasn't sure if he was nervous about his friends' reaction to Margot or vice versa. Probably both.

He took her hand and walked her to the door. Bill and Terry smiled at him, then both men focused on Margot. Bill shook her hand, introducing himself, and Terry handed her a bottle of wine.

"Thank you," she said, tugging Daniel back so the two men could enter the apartment. "So you're the crew from Rutgers, huh? I insist that you both get sloshed tonight and tell me all of Daniel's horribly embarrassing secrets."

"No problem," Bill said. "We like doing that. In fact, we've been known to stop strangers in the street just to tell them something stupid Houghton pulled."

"Excellent." Margot smiled brilliantly. "I'm going to take along this fine wine when we go to our first stop. I assume you know the deal?"

"Revolving dinner," Terry said. "Never done it, seen it on the Food Channel."

"We're not as sophisticated as a gourmet club," Margot said. "Mostly we'll eat anything as long as we can have wine to go with it."

"Works for me," Bill said.

"Okay then." Margot put the wine down on the coffee table. "I've got to finish getting my act together. You boys play nice, and give me about ten minutes, okay?"

Three nods followed her as she walked to the bedroom. Daniel realized, without doubt, what precisely his friends were looking at as they watched her go. It was a very nice view.

"So," Terry said, sitting down on the nearest couch. "You *have* been abducted by aliens."

"What are you talking about?" Daniel sat down across from him. The guys had dressed as requested in jeans and casual shirts. Bill looked as if he'd dropped a few pounds and gotten some rest.

"Look at you. What the hell kind of shirt is that?"

"Fashionable," Daniel said.

"My point," Terry said. "And get a load of that haircut."

Bill laughed. "He's right, old man. You're looking vaguely like you fit in the twenty-first century."

"Gee, thanks."

"Nope, it's a compliment," Bill said, checking out the view to the balcony. "And your taste in women has improved, too."

Daniel grinned. "You like?"

"Hell, yeah." Bill turned. "What I don't get is what she's doing with a stick like you."

"Hey."

"Come on, man." Terry leaned forward, putting his elbows on his knees. "I've met your other women. She ain't one of 'em."

"That's right, she's not."

"Not complaining. Just surprised, that's all."

Daniel stood. "Yeah, well, there's a lot that's changed since I moved here. Not just my taste in women."

Bill meandered to the other couch, his gaze doing a quick inventory of the room. "Ah, that explains it."

"Explains what?"

"I heard something about you, my boy," Bill went on as he sat down.

"What?"

"Seems you're causing a little stir at the office."

"How in hell would you know?"

Bill looked at Terry, then back at Daniel. "That new office you're working on? Johnson is my CPA."

That was news to Daniel. He had never asked Bill about the details of his finances. "What has he said?"

"That the preliminary drawings weren't what they expected."

Daniel sat back. "What they expected was the most boring piece of crap you can imagine."

"Danny boy, these guys are accountants. They live for boring."

"Yeah, well, I'm just trying to give them some options, okay?"

"Just don't forget why they came to you, buddy."

Daniel was about to retort when Margot came back into the room. He couldn't see that anything had changed while she was in the other room, but the ways of women were still a mystery to him. All he knew was that she looked great, and that he was damn ready to change the subject.

"I'm set. You guys ready to have a wonderful dinner?"

All three men stood. Daniel grabbed the wine bottle and Margot's hand. "Let's go."

As they went to the door, Margot gave him a questioning look, which he ignored. He just hoped trying to mix his two worlds wasn't a huge mistake.

15

MARGOT SURVEYED HER DOMAIN. All the basic ingredients to make a Whompies pizza were there, but there were miles to go. She had pizza shells, lots of them. Because this commercial would need a pull, where the cheese has to stretch, she had to cut the slice first, then put it back in and pin it to the crust.

There was a ton of mozzarella to be shredded, sauce to be drained, pepperoni to be sliced and microwaved, onions, peppers and tomatoes to be sliced and treated. After that, the real work would begin.

And here she was, all alone, again, at five in the morning. D and G hadn't gotten her more help. She was stuck with the magnificently inept Bettina and Rick. Who, even if they did manage to do something right, did it in slow motion. So Margot would have to prep, then bake, then style. Which was a bitch on a pizza, especially a pepperoni pull.

She should just quit. Who else would have put up with this nonsense? But instead, she tied on her apron and got to work.

As she shredded, she thought about the dinner last night. She'd really liked Daniel's friends. Especially Bill. Mostly because he'd kept Corrie laughing all through the extended meal. Bless his heart, he'd taken a shine to her friend, who'd really needed the boost. For a few hours at least, Corrie hadn't thought about Nels, or her tenuous situation.

That was another thing Margot was going to do today. Talk to the AD and see if there were any jobs available. And then she'd call Janice at the ad firm.

She finished the first pound of cheese, and then switched over to onions, slicing them as carefully and evenly as she could. They would then go into plastic bags, then into the fridge. She couldn't do the tomatoes until the last minute, but after the onions she'd drain the sauce, then come back and do more cheese.

For the next hour, in the quiet of the empty stage, she busied herself with her prep. She worked slowly, making sure every step was done with care and precision. And she thought about Daniel.

She had a decision to make about him, and she needed to make it soon. Saturday night was her cousin Estelle's wedding. She wanted to take Daniel, which would be heaven because they could get dressed up and dance and drink and be silly, and perhaps even stay in a hotel room. On the other hand, it would mean introducing him to her family.

She really liked Daniel, and she didn't want him to run screaming onto the streets of Great Neck in a rented tuxedo. That would be very bad.

Somehow she had the feeling he'd never been to a Jewish wedding. Even if he had, it hadn't been with her loony relatives.

There was her older-than-God uncle Moe, who

started off every story in English, segued to Yiddish and ended in Russian. No one had understood the man since 1992. Her aunt Ida, who stole anything she could get her hands on and stuffed it in a carpetbag the size of Ohio. They were only the tip of the iceberg, with Estelle, the bride, the most bizarre piece of work of all. She made Janice from *Friends* seem like Diane Sawyer.

But maybe he'd just think they were all charmingly eccentric. He probably had crazy relatives, too. Not the same kind of crazy, but she could always hope he had some uncle who wore ladies' panties.

No, it would be too weird. Her mother would give him the third degree, want to know what his prospects were, and if he could believe what the caterers were charging for lox. Her father would try and get him to invest in an eBay scheme, and then her cousin Tina would hit on him after her second martini.

Her phone rang, and since she was always prepared with her little earphone, she just stuck her hand in her apron pocket and turned the phone on. "Margot, Girl Genius."

"Hi, Margot, Girl Genius."

She smiled, feeling squishy and warm all over. "Oh, you must be that handsome devil that's always hanging out on the third floor."

"That's me."

She tossed her hair, then remembered it was in a bun. "So how come you're up so early, my gorgeous lust bunny?"

"Because you drive me crazy."

Her grin grew to idiot size. "I do?"

"Yes. You do."

"And are we going to share the particulars?"

"I can still smell you." His voice sounded sleepy, and dreamy.

"Are you in bed?"

"Uh-huh."

"Are you naked?"

He laughed. "You know me too well."

"Oh, sure. Call me up to taunt me with your naked-ness while I'm knee-deep in mozzarella balls."

"Isn't there somewhere private around there?"

"I suppose."

"So?"

She giggled. "It sounds like you're busy with *your* balls."

"I think I should be insulted."

"Now, now. We both know you have a very hefty sau-sage and two juicy meatballs."

He laughed. "Somehow, when I dialed your number, this wasn't the conversation I pictured."

"Well, I am a food stylist. Sometimes I get carried away."

"You're also the most luscious, sexy, fantastic woman I've ever met."

She sighed. "Okay, you win. I'm going to the ladies' room."

"Are you going to get naked, too?"

"No. I'm at my place of employment. They usually prefer their food handlers to keep their clothes on."

"They're idiots."

She headed out of her kitchen across the dark, empty

sound stage. "So, tell me what you were thinking about before dialing."

"Mmm. Well, you were there."

"I'm flattered."

"I was there."

"Always good."

"And there was no cheese at all."

"Phew." She got to the ladies' rest room and ducked inside. Figuring it would be okay while no one was around, she chose the handicapped stall. More maneuvering room. She locked the stall. "What else?" she asked, leaning against the wall.

"I was just remembering that night."

"Which night?"

"The night where we did…stuff."

"Ah, stuff."

He chuckled. "Great stuff."

"You're a kinky bastard, aren't you?"

"You know, I never thought so, but I'm beginning to see things a little differently."

"Oh?"

"Uh-huh. Because I was thinking about you, on the bed, spread-eagled."

"But?"

"But this time, you're not on your back."

That stopped her. She blinked as her cheeks heated. "Not on my back?"

"Nope. You're on your tummy."

"And where are you?"

"I'm running my fingers down your beautiful shoulders."

She closed her eyes, imagining the sensation. "And?"

"Kissing the small of your back."

"Oh."

She heard the soft shuffle of sheets moving. It had been so difficult to leave him this morning. He'd been curled around her, his leg over hers, his arm around her waist. He hadn't even stirred when the alarm went off.

"And now I'm kissing lower."

Her eyebrows went up. "Oh!"

"Uh-huh."

"You are a kinky bastard."

"I told you. I'm becoming a new man. Daring. Adventurous."

"I like adventurous."

"Good, because I haven't even gotten to the good stuff yet."

"Oh."

"You in private yet?"

"Uh-huh."

She turned away from the door, which on some level she knew was moronic, then untied the back of her apron. With it still around her neck, she touched her breast, not in the least surprised to find her nipple was hard enough to cut glass. "I'm touching myself."

"Good."

"What are you doing now?"

"I'm moving down."

"Oh, right. Down."

He chuckled again, but she could hear his breath was coming more rapidly. "Down."

"And what is it, exactly, that you plan to do in this very interesting position?"

"First, I'm going to explore you with my hands."

"Ah."

"You like that?"

"You have wonderful hands, Daniel."

"Thank you. But I think you're going to like my tongue better."

She squeezed her legs together. Moved her hands down the front of her shirt to the waistband of her skirt.

"Oh, God," he said, his voice straining. "I kiss your beautiful hip, but I can't help it. I have to taste more."

She made a sound, which had started out as a word, then dissolved, like her promise that she wouldn't let this get out of hand.

"I bite you. Your body arches and you make that sound I love so much."

"What sound?"

"That little yelp. It makes me insane."

Her hand was under her skirt now, and heading toward the band of her panties. "More," she whispered.

His breathing was really hard now, as hard as she imagined him to be. Behind her closed eyes she could picture his beautiful erection, so thick and long…

"Touch yourself," he whispered thickly, his voice low and rough as nubby silk. "I want to hear you come."

"I…"

"Please, baby. Come for me. I'm nipping at your soft, round flesh, moving away from your hip, letting my fingers trace that forbidden line that hides your secrets."

She was there now. Her fingers brushing against her moist lower lips, aching to do as he asked.

He moaned, long and deep.

She slipped her finger into her own moist fold.

"Margot," he said, his voice desperate, close.

"Daniel…"

"Baby, please…"

"I'm almost—"

"Oh, God!"

And then the bathroom door slammed open. Margot screamed, yanking her hand out so hard she nearly ripped her own panties. Disconnecting her phone call. But not before she heard Daniel's agonized howl.

DANIEL HAD BEEN WORKING at the design all afternoon, and nothing was coming out right. He had so many ideas, none of which, he knew, would fly with the client. He couldn't believe the tension in his shoulders, the headache that had come on just after noon. He threw his drafting pencil on his desk and got up. His walk to the window felt so good he decided he needed to get outside. Try to work off some of this crap, get his head in order.

Jill was behind the big desk in the reception area, and he told her he'd be back in a half hour. She nodded, smiled, checked him out, which she'd taken to doing ever since that day he'd come in with his new haircut. She never said anything about it, never asked why he'd returned to his old habits, but there was something a little challenging in her stare.

He went out to the street, surprised that it was so cool. For summer, that is. But today there was an actual breeze and the humidity wasn't unbearable. Now spring was something else. Blooming flowers, billowing clouds and even the crowded streets had a kind of hope in them. Today was like that, but it was just a brief respite. He tried like hell to get out of the city for at least a few weeks every August.

Maybe he and Margot could go somewhere. A bed-and-breakfast in the Hamptons. Or maybe a cottage on Martha's Vineyard. It would be great to have some time to just relax and play, not worry about work, hers or his. He knew she was having a hard time with that director on the Whompies.

She'd outlined her five-year plan to him, and it made a great deal of sense, but she didn't go into the details.

Anyway, who was he to offer career advice? Just look at the box he'd gotten himself into. He walked to the huge building that was next to his office, through the lobby to the courtyard. There were benches, flower boxes, running water with a great fountain right in the middle. He often came there to eat lunch, as did lots of other people, but he was lucky and found an empty bench near enough to the fountain that he could be soothed by the sound.

He sat down, wondering when he started to think of himself as being trapped. He'd used to like his work, his job. There'd been comfort in the familiar, and he understood the need his clients had for a sense of continuity and strength in the buildings that represented their attitudes. When had it changed?

With Margot, of course. So much had. She'd opened his eyes to so much. His own sense of style, the narrow scope of his vision. All the things he'd assumed were written in stone were being etched away, leaving clean slates in their wake.

Which most of the time filled him with a sense of excitement. But sometimes, particularly when he thought about work, scared him.

He remembered what Bill had said last night. That the changes were starting to show. The question was, did he care? Major things were at risk here, and up until a few months ago, he'd never dreamed of stepping outside of his own life plan. Work at Kogen, Teasdale and Webster, make partner, then do a little experimenting on the side. He'd have financial security, a steady foundation for a family. His hobby designs were always enough to keep his creativity stimulated, and it all seemed eminently practical.

But eminently practical had lost a lot of its appeal.

The thing was, he'd never, not since college, and maybe not even then, felt so damn alive. With Margot, he could do anything, be anyone. Dare to risk. At least that's how it felt when he was with her. But in the warm light of day, his bravado slipped. The old ways of thinking came back to pull him to his office, to force his hand to draw the same old same old. Then he'd be back in her arms, and he wanted to stop being a geek and turn into superhero.

And yet, he'd done nothing about it. Yeah, he'd given the clients a bit of a shock with some ideas that weren't exactly radical, but not within the conventional framework. He'd thrown caution to the wind and worn a damn shirt for all of one day. Then he'd crawled back meekly into safety.

Is that what he wanted? Safety? He had some money. Not enough to retire on, but say he did go crazy, he wouldn't starve or lose his place for at least a year.

Just thinking about it made him more nervous than he cared to admit. Shit. He'd never thought of himself as a coward, but maybe that's exactly what he was. He'd never even had the guts to show anyone his personal designs. Until Margot, of course.

What must she think of him, going to his dull job day after day, molding himself to fit into the conservative box he'd built. Here she was approaching her life with fierce determination and grit.

He sighed, watching a man smoke a cigarette. He looked furious at the world, or maybe himself. Probably compromised one too many times.

Daniel felt like walking back into Edgar's office and handing him his resignation. But, there were some lessons from his father that weren't so easily dismissed. Do nothing in the heat of the moment. Take a step back. Examine your options. Don't shoot yourself in the foot.

Okay, so he wouldn't do anything crazy. He'd talk it over with the guys. They knew him well and would give him their honest opinions. And he'd talk to Margot. Of course.

His cell rang, and he flipped it open. "Houghton."

"Hi, Houghton."

He felt instantly better at the sound of her voice. "Hey."

"Sorry about this morning."

"That was quite some climax. You nearly perforated my eardrum."

"Someone came in the bathroom."

"I hope it was you."

"Cute. And don't worry. They just thought I was nuts, not a pervert."

"Well, thank God."

"I felt bad, hanging up like that."

"Don't worry about it. Actually, it was pretty dramatic."

She chuckled, and he shifted on the warm bench, wishing she were here. "How would you like to be my date at my cousin's wedding on Saturday night?"

"Sure."

"Wait, don't answer so quickly. It means meeting my family."

"Sure."

"*My* family. Did I not make that clear?"

"Margot, I'd love to go. I'm looking forward to it."

She was silent for so long he checked that they were still connected. Then finally, she asked, "Have you ever been to a Jewish wedding?"

"I saw *Fiddler on the Roof,* does that count?"

"Oh, dear."

"Hey, how bad could it be?"

Her laughter made him nervous. Real nervous.

16

DANIEL FELT MARGOT SLOW as they reached the doors of the Long Island hotel ballroom. He looked at her, wondering why she seemed so hesitant. He touched the back of her neck as he leaned close to her ear. "You're the most beautiful woman here."

"You haven't even gone in."

"Doesn't matter. I know it's true."

The smile she gave him made it worth renting the tux, the car, everything. What made it even better was that he was telling her the truth. She looked stunning. Her pale gray dress caressed her body as he wanted to, hugging her in all the right places. She smelled like the most perfect flower, and her face just glowed. God, he wanted to skip the damn wedding and make love to her for the rest of the night. She'd probably jump at the offer, but he'd promised. "Come on, let's do it."

She held up her hand, stepped away from him and looked him over from head to toe.

"What's wrong?"

Her gaze came up to meet his. "Absolutely nothing." Then she grinned.

"What?"

"There's only one thing that could make you more beautiful."

He arched his eyebrow, waiting.

Again she held up her hand, asked him to wait as she entered the ballroom, but she was only gone for a few seconds. She came back with something dark in her hand.

"What is it?"

"Required."

"But what is it?"

"A yarmulke."

"Ah."

"Ever wear one before?"

"Actually, yes. I'm not totally ignorant of your foreign ways, missy. I've been to a bar mitzvah."

"Wow."

"And how many baptisms have you attended?"

"Touché," she said, as she put the small skullcap on the crown of his head, affixing it with a dark bobby pin. Then she stepped back and sighed. "The handsomest man here."

He took her hand and went inside the room. Which was huge, and filled with tables. Elaborately decorated in pale pink and lavender, it was like something out of a movie. He'd only been to one wedding this fancy before, and it was for some relative of the Rockefellers. A huge banquet lined two walls, there were four bars, a sixteen-piece orchestra and flowers everywhere.

The attendees looked like wedding guests are supposed to, uncomfortable and hungry. But no one was eating.

There was a small table at the head of the room, just below the bandstand. On it was one of the largest loaves of braided bread he'd ever seen, and a golden goblet.

"That's for the *bracha*."

"The what?"

"The blessing," Margot said. "Estelle's father will give it, then we can eat."

"How long do we have to wait?"

"Not long."

The band started playing some old standards from the seventies, and he had to admit, for music he didn't care for, they were pretty good.

Margot brought him to a corner where there weren't many people and started pointing out relatives and family friends. He'd never keep them all straight, there were just too many. Most everyone seemed to know each other, and the two of them got a lot of stares.

Finally, a couple about their age approached. The woman, who was extremely thin with very round, large breasts, approached, her arms held out. "Margot! My God, it's been forever." The woman perfunctorily hugged Margot, then turned her attention to him. "And who is this?"

"Daniel." She turned to him with a look of utter dread. "Daniel, this is Tina."

"Nice to meet you," Tina said, moving in for a kiss on the cheek which lingered a little too long. When she finally stepped back, she vaguely waved at the man beside her. "Elliot."

The man, who looked as if he'd picked up the wrong tux, stuck out his hand, and Daniel shook it. "So, when's this shindig gonna start?"

"Hush," Tina said, never taking her eyes from Daniel's. "I haven't seen you at one of these functions before."

"I've never been invited."

"An oversight, I'm sure."

Her accent, Brooklyn or Queens, he could never tell the difference, was thick as April mud.

Margot grabbed his hand. "There's my folks. See you later, Tina." And then they were away. Fast.

"That was interesting," he said, as they headed across the room.

"She hasn't even begun. Wait till she gets drunk."

"Speaking of which…" He steered her toward the bar. "What would you like?"

"About six shots of tequila, with beer chasers, but I'll take a white wine."

"Got it." They stood in the short line, while he looked in the direction she'd been pulling him. "Which ones are your parents?"

"See the woman in the blue dress standing next to the bald guy who's talking to himself?"

He followed her finger until he found them. Margot's mother was attractive, too, which didn't surprise him. Older, plumper, but he could see where the exotic looks came from. Her father seemed distracted and ready to leave, but as he watched, her mother reached over and straightened his tie. The smiles between them had a warmth that was palpable. He'd never seen anything remotely like it between his parents.

"Sir?"

He turned back to the bartender and got their drinks. Before he could hand Margot hers, she reached over and straightened his tie. The smile she gave him made him swallow hard. Then, as if it had been nothing, she got her drink and his hand.

Just as they reached her parents, the lights dimmed and the microphone squealed. Everyone turned to the front of the room. An older man stood in front of the small table and started speaking Hebrew. Daniel didn't understand a word, but he kind of liked the ritualistic aspect of it all. The lifting of the wine cup, the chanting singsong of the prayer. The man ate a bit of bread, sipped a bit of wine, and then everyone said, "Amen." Then he gave a short toast to the bride and groom, who were sitting on what he could only describe as thrones, and invited everyone to enjoy the night.

Margot introduced him to her parents, who studied him with open curiosity. He smiled, feeling as if he had something big stuck between his teeth.

"So, you're an architect?" her mother asked.

"That's right."

"A good business."

"I enjoy it."

"And you make a good living?"

Margot moaned softly beside him.

"I do all right."

"That's good. You must make your parents proud."

"I think they're pleased."

Daniel couldn't help notice that most of the people in the room were in line for the buffet, and that Margot's father was staring at the food. Daniel offered his arm to her mother. "Shall we get in line, Mrs. Janowitz?"

She put her hand regally on his tux sleeve. "Why thank you. And call me Bernice."

Daniel looked back at Margot and got a surreptitious

thumbs-up. Then she grabbed her father's hand and they got in line.

By the time they had walked the length of the table, his plate was piled high, courtesy of Bernice. She told him what everything was. He even recognized some of it, but then there were things like *cholent*, a Sabbath stew made of meat, beans and potatoes and *griven*, fried pieces of chicken skin, that were out of his taste league. He just kept smiling and nodding.

They ended up standing too close to the band, having to shout at each other to be heard. He found it easier to eat, which he managed even while standing. Bernice nibbled, but she preferred to talk. And talk. Mostly about Margot, but she asked him a lot of questions. He almost spit when she mentioned that if he and Margot should get married he'd have to convert.

Deftly dodging that bullet by asking her about the store she used to own, he was incredibly grateful when Margot came, disposed of their plates, and took him away.

"Was it horrible?"

"Not at all."

"Come on, Daniel. She's my mother. I know."

"Honestly, she was great."

"So she didn't sign you up for the conversion classes at Temple Beth Israel?"

He laughed. "Another two minutes…"

"I warned you."

He stopped her halfway onto the dance floor. Pulled her into his arms. "I'm fine."

She smiled up at him. "Thank you again."

"For what?"

"For being such a mensch."

"I'm a prince. A sweetheart," he said, in a self-deprecating tone of voice.

"You *are*."

"I don't imagine you speak much Episcopalian, so I guess it's all right."

She laughed. "You know, some people around us are moving. To the music. It's called dancing."

"No kidding?"

She shook her head as she raked her nails down his back. He hadn't even noticed when she'd slipped her hands under his coat. He pulled her tighter, kissed her lips gently, then started to move. Not just move. He danced.

Margot's eyes widened.

"Surprised?"

"My God, you're a virtual Fred Astaire. I'm definitely outclassed."

"Three years at Mrs. Ellison's Etiquette and Ballroom."

"You must have been at the top of your class."

"I hated every moment of it, but what can I say? It had to be done."

She rested her head against his chest. "Well, slow down, Fred, I can't keep up."

He stopped showing off and just enjoyed the closeness. The bride and groom were dancing nearby, and he watched them for a while. But they didn't seem all that transported by marital bliss, so he closed his eyes and buried his face in Margot's hair.

An hour later, they came back to the dance floor. This

time, Daniel wasn't so light on his feet, and Margot cracked up all over again.

He paused. "What?"

"I can't believe you ate all those hors d'oeuvres."

"How was I supposed to know that layout wasn't the meal? Jeez."

"Poor baby."

"It's fine. I'm fine. But, uh, how long do these things usually last?"

"Forever."

"Oh."

She chuckled, moving with him so easily to the sounds of "Moon River." "Don't worry. We'll make our escape soon."

"I want to get you alone. Have I told you how beautiful you look tonight?"

"Uh-huh."

"Well, it's true."

"I had to look good. All these other women are trying to steal you away."

He laughed.

She pulled her head back. "You haven't noticed?"

"What are you talking about?"

She laughed. "You are so pretty."

"Hey."

"I mean that in the nicest possible way."

He sighed, pulled her close again. "Is it time yet?"

She nodded against his chest. "Let's dance to the door."

He headed that way. And they would have made it, if it hadn't been for the wedding cake.

The thing was huge, five tiers, all white and pink and

lavender. Margot pulled Daniel to the side of the room, but they couldn't leave just yet, not with so many lights blaring.

He'd been so good. So nice. He'd talked to pretty much every one of her relatives without complaint. He'd even been nice to Moishe, who was the biggest ass this side of the Mississippi. And he'd complimented her mother, listened to her father, and even danced with her aunt Sadie. He really was a peach. Not to mention the most gorgeous man here. By a hell of a lot.

She had no idea how she'd gotten so lucky. And how much longer she could fool herself into thinking this was just sex and friendship.

His hand tugged hers gently, moving her backward. She went, not looking around, just following where he would lead. While the bride fed the groom his piece of cake, Daniel sneaked her out the door, dropping his yarmulke in the box on the way. Then they ran. Like kids. Well, almost, because most kids don't wear three-inch heels, but they sure giggled like the real thing.

They rushed toward the lobby, but Daniel's arm caught her around the waist and he yanked her sideways so suddenly she yelped. They were in the elevator alcove. Alone.

He leaned her against the hard marble wall and kissed her. Deeply, his tongue darting and thrusting, moaning as his hands went behind her back. Which was a good thing, because her knees had grown incredibly weak. Just watching Daniel walk around in that Armani tux had been intoxicating. Now to be in his arms, to feel his desperation and need pressing against her…

The ding of the elevator pulled him away. She tried to get her act together, but that was useless. No one was there anyway. Until Daniel led her inside. He pushed the button for the eighteenth floor.

"What are you doing?"

He gave her a brilliant smile as he held his hands up. "Surprise."

"Are you kidding?"

"You want to go home? We can go. I just thought…

She grabbed him by his lapels and pulled him to her. "You are—"

"Wonderful? Considerate? A great dancer?"

She put her finger to his lips. "Astonishing."

"Nah. Astonishing is all the crap your aunt Ida gets into that purse. I expected her to pull out a Boeing 707."

Margot kissed the bottom of his chin. "We all think it's where she hid my uncle Frank. No one ever saw the body."

He ran his knuckle down the side of her face. "Thank you."

"For what?"

"Inviting me here tonight."

"Please. Stop being so nice. I don't know how to handle it. I'm used to shitty boyfriends."

His eyebrows came down along with his smile. "Who was shitty to you? I'll kill him."

"I know. And that's another thing I love about you."

The right eyebrow came up. High. "Another? There are other things you love about me?"

Love? Had she actually said that? It was a figure of speech. That's all. But then, he didn't look upset, so maybe…

She was saved from her own breathlessness by the stopping of the elevator.

He led her down the hall to 1814 and produced a key from his pocket.

"When?"

"Bathroom."

"Ah."

"Second time."

"I thought—"

"Nope. Key."

"Excellent."

"Shut up and get in here."

She did. And gaped. It wasn't a room, it was a suite, and it was gorgeous. Of course Estelle wouldn't have her wedding in any other place but the best hotel in Great Neck, but this was way better than Margot expected. Flowers on the wet bar, furniture she would consider for her own home. Okay, for a friend's home, but still. Stunning.

Of course she had to see the bedroom, and the huge billowy bed was definitely California King. She turned to find Daniel leaning against the door frame, his arms crossed over his chest, a very satisfied grin on his face. "It's—"

"Wonderful? Extravagant?"

"Precisely."

"Can I just say one thing?"

She nodded.

"You have too many clothes on."

She stepped back. Arched her eyebrows. Put the back of her hand to her cheek. "So this was all a come-on? You did all this just to get me in bed?"

"Well, yeah."

"Oh, thank God." She reached behind her back and pulled down her zipper. Let her gorgeous dress pool at her feet. Then she looked at him sternly. "Waiting for an engraved invitation?"

He shook his head slowly. "Just let me enjoy this, okay? Then I'll do whatever you want."

"Whatever?"

He nodded, just as seriously.

She flipped one bra strap down her shoulder. "Then you might want to get comfy, 'cause honey, I'm going to make this good."

MARGOT COULD SEE HIS FACE in the light of the moon. That wonderful moon. He was sleeping, and she should be, too. It was almost three in the morning, and the things he'd done to her…

She shivered, remembering the feel of him inside her. The way his tongue had made her tremble. She'd never known it could be like this. Not even close.

The thing was, and it was completely and utterly useless to deny it, she'd gone and fallen in love. Bigtime. Deeply, completely and all the way. The thought of not being with Daniel was unbearable. When she wasn't with him, she wanted to be. When she was, all the rest of the world could disappear, and she wouldn't notice, let alone care.

So much for friendship and sex. Not that they didn't have both those things, but she'd caught the bullet train past that weeks ago. Maybe longer.

Which begged the question, what now? Tell him?

He'd never said anything close to the *L* word. And frankly, if he didn't…she wasn't sure she could take it.

She let her head fall back to the pillow, but sleep didn't come.

17

DANIEL STARED at his finished design. It was just what the client wanted. Sturdy, elegant, totally within the budget. He hated it. He hated that he'd had to dedicate three months of his life to this boring crap. Hated that he'd boxed himself into this stuffy corner, with no way out.

He shoved his tablet off the table and reached for his portfolio. From there, he brought out the drawings he'd done at home. Mostly late at night, when Margot had needed her sleep and he'd left her to it.

He studied the design for the outside front of the building. It wasn't far out, not the least bit futuristic like his dream projects, but it wasn't that horrible box the client had asked for. It was almost Gothic, but with modern details. He could so clearly picture it, the way the etched doors would reflect the light, how the windows would seem like eyes to the city.

Turning the page, he examined the lobby. Damn, it was a thing of beauty. Practical, yet this elegance was in the form and function, and there wasn't a picture of a fox or a hound in sight. The water feature was the focal point, and a meandering stream that led clients to the inner recesses. It would soothe and comfort, relax anyone in the foyer as they waited to discuss their tax problems.

But there was something wrong with the front desk, and he absently grabbed his pencil to fix it. As he redesigned, he made his decision. The presentation was in two hours.

If they couldn't see the beauty of this building, then screw 'em.

MARGOT STOOD BEHIND the food-services table and debated the wisdom of eating all the doughnuts in the box. She probably shouldn't, but eating a couple of dozen sweets might just put her into a diabetic coma, and that would be better than standing here listening to the director complain about what a lousy stylist she was.

She was back with Whompies for the third of four shoots. Why, she had no idea. She'd tried so damn hard. Given it everything she had, and still she wasn't able to give them what they wanted. At this point she didn't even know what they wanted. To her eye, the food looked exactly right. Just like in all the other Whompie commercials. Juicy when it was supposed to be, succulent, toasty, fizzy, leafy, hard, soft. It wasn't her fault that she was always late. It took the time it took. Shit. She'd never expected this. This was supposed to be a piece of cake, something she could do in her sleep. And she was utterly miserable at it.

She thought about her last assignment, the one for the pretzel catalog. That had been fun and interesting. Who'd have thought. Pretzels. But the art director had been a blast, he'd let her play to her heart's content, and frankly, she'd been brilliant. Nothing like this. Of course that was print, not television. Evidently, she sucked at TV. Which made her life plan kind of a moot point, yes?

"Margot."

She turned at the voice, the touch to her arm. "Corrie? What are you doing here?"

"Is it okay? I can leave if you want."

"Of course it's okay, but let's go to the kitchen. More privacy."

Margot led Corrie through the maze of lights and cables and people until they were behind the prep kitchen door. Then she looked at the marvelously animated face of her best friend. She looked years younger, happier than she'd seen her in ages. "What? Tell me before I have a stroke."

Corrie flashed her a killer smile. "I got a job."

"No."

"Yes."

First came the hug, a major one, then came the details.

"You'll never guess who got it for me."

"Who?"

"Bill."

"Daniel's Bill?"

She nodded.

Margot went to the fridge and pulled out two cans of soda. She set them down at the table where they both sat in mismatched chairs, huddled close.

"Tell me every last detail," Margot said. "Have you been talking to him all this time?"

Corrie nodded. "He's a sweetheart. Drinks too much, but hey, who wouldn't in his shoes?"

"Huh?"

"Kidding. Anyway, a few days ago he called and told me about this company that he owns. Owns, Margot, like in owns."

"Oh, my."

"Yeah. Argell Corporation. They make cosmetics for all kinds of name labels. Anyway, one of the divisions, Dawn, needs a regional rep for the Eastern seaboard."

"Sales?"

She nodded. "It would mean almost a month of training in their facilities in Raleigh. Then I'd go to major department stores and do sales and demonstrations. Salary plus commission, full benefits, and oh, my God, a company car."

"You can't drive."

"I'll learn."

Margot sat back in her chair. "This is terrific."

"I know."

"And it's really yours?"

"I think he fixed it because, I gotta tell you, the interview was not the shining highlight of my life. But they called an hour ago, and I had to come and tell you."

"Have you talked to Bill?"

"He wasn't around, but I left a message."

"When do you start?"

"I fly to Raleigh on Sunday."

"Oh, God. That's like, Sunday."

Corrie laughed. "Yeah. But that's not all."

Margot popped the top of her soda and took a big drink. "There's more?"

"I'm telling Nels. Tonight."

"About the job?"

"About the divorce."

Margot's elation deflated. She reached to take Corrie's hand. "Are you sure about this?"

"Yeah, I'm sure. I just can't do it anymore. I'm tired of feeling like I'm wrong. I'm tired of seeing that look of disgust on his face when he thinks I can't see him. I'm tired of smelling another woman's perfume on his jacket."

"What happens when you get back from Raleigh?"

"He should be moved out by then."

"So you're asking him to leave?"

"He doesn't love the building like I do. He has no friends there. And he can afford the move."

"Can you afford the place by yourself?"

"It's going to be tough, but with the new job…"

"This is the best. The absolute best. I was so afraid I was going to lose you."

"Me? Move from the miracle that is our building? Not likely."

Margot held up her hand as she thought she heard someone calling her from the stage, but she didn't hear it again. "Is the job the only thing that's cropped up with Bill?"

Corrie rolled her eyes. "You have a terminally filthy mind."

"Yes, I do. Now answer me."

"So far, yes."

"But?"

"But I think he's interested in more."

"Have you gone out with him?"

"Twice."

"And you didn't tell me?"

Corrie blinked at her. "You've been very busy, kiddo."

Margot could only nod. "Sorry about that."

"I'll forgive you if you tell me what's going on with you and Daniel. No one ever sees you guys any more. Although we do hear you occasionally when walking by your door."

"Oh."

"Yeah."

"Things are great." She sipped more soda, then looked at the can.

"But?" Corrie said, studying her face too carefully.

"I'm in pretty deep."

"How deep?"

"All the way to China deep."

"Oh."

"Yeah."

Corrie leaned in, cupping her soda can. "And he is?"

"Happy. Content. Friendship and sex. What more could he want?"

"You?"

"He's got me."

"Are you sure he doesn't want the same thing you do? Maybe he just thinks all you want is the whole F and S thing."

"I would know if he did."

"Because you're a renowned psychic?"

"Because I'd just…know."

"Idiot."

"Excuse me?"

"I said you're an idiot. Talk to the guy. Tell him what's going on."

"I'm not…"

"What?"

She didn't know exactly what she wasn't. "I don't know. I'm just not."

"He's crazy about you. It's written all over him. He adores you."

"I know he likes me. And he was so good at the wedding. Oh, my God. Did you know he can dance? Seriously dance?"

"Margot, honey, you have to say something."

"Why?"

"Because if you don't, it's going to get all weird and you'll do something to chase him away."

"What are you talking about?"

"It's me, Corrie. I know you."

"Know what?"

"That you're a lot more comfortable with bad than good. And if it's good for too long, you'll make it bad."

Margot felt that all the way to her heart. All the way back to Gordon and beyond. "I'm pathetic."

"No, you're not. It's just time to move forward. Do it differently. And you couldn't do it with a better guy than Daniel."

"Weren't you the one that said I was trying to change him into something he's not? What happened to all that?"

Corrie shook her head. "I don't know. I can only tell you what I see. He doesn't seem to mind, so why should I? I think you two are good for each other, and it would be a shame to screw it up. Of course, I'm a woman leaving a miserable marriage, so what do I know?"

"Me," Margot said softly.

The door swung open, and Margot's chest tightened

as she saw who was there. It wasn't the director, it was Janice Freedman, the vice president of Galloway and Donnelly. Not even glancing at Corrie, she came up to the table and faced Margot with an expression as if she just smelled burned toast.

Margot stood up. "Janice."

"Margot, we have an issue here."

"Oh?"

"The footage has been good. In the main, Whompies is happy. But there are problems."

"What would those be?"

"You're costing too much. Taking too much time. The tacos took an entire day and most of the negative budget. Bert didn't think the pizza worked and he wants to reshoot it."

"The pizza? It was gorgeous."

"He said it wasn't cheesy enough."

Margot tried to stop her heart from hammering, her hands from shaking. This was every nightmare she'd ever had, every personal insecurity run up the tallest flagpole. She wanted the floor to open up and swallow her whole.

"Look," Janice said, her perfect Prada suit shifting subtly as she leaned closer. "Your print work is fantastic. We all love it. Maybe we should just stick to that."

"Janice, you know they didn't give me enough support. I told you that from the beginning. Give me a proper team and I can do this. I can give them what they want. There's only three days left. Let me finish."

"I don't see how I can get the budget to give you more people."

"You and I both know what shoots like this require. If you meet me halfway, I'll make it perfect. Just give me one more chance. Please, Janice. You know I can."

"That's the problem, Margot. I don't. But I'll see what I can do."

Margot tried to get some air into her lungs. "Thank you."

Janice, who was about three inches shorter than Margot, looked up at her with the most lifeless eyes she'd ever seen. "Try harder," she said, then she turned and walked out, her heels clicking on the concrete floor.

Margot felt Corrie's hand on her shoulder, but she shook it off. Without looking at her friend, she turned to the fridge. "I'm sorry, I have to get back to work."

"Okay," Corrie said, her voice achingly soft. "I'll call you later."

Margot nodded, willing herself not to cry.

DANIEL LOOKED AROUND the room, freezing as he fixed on Edgar. His face was pasty, and there was sweat on his upper lip. In fact, Edgar looked as if he was about to have a heart attack. Daniel tried to reassure him with a smile, but he failed.

The presentation had been the best of his life. He'd been on top of his game. Everything he'd pitched had been from the heart, and he'd known, just known, that he was winning them over.

Clearly, he'd been delusional. No one was sold, no one was smiling, no one was even blinking.

What the hell had he done? He'd just committed professional suicide, that's what. These people didn't want his ideas. They didn't want anything new. They wanted comfort. Continuity. The same building they were moving from, only bigger.

"Thank you, Daniel," his boss said. "Perhaps now would be a time to present the primary designs."

Daniel nodded. "Absolutely. Why don't we take a five-minute break and then proceed." He didn't wait for a response, instead, he fled the conference room as fast as possible without actually running, straight for his office to regroup. Now. Damn it, he was a moron. But there was a chance he could save the account. He gathered his materials then held on to the back of his chair as a wave of vertigo nearly knocked him on his ass.

This was nuts, he knew better than this. God, all he could think about was getting home to Margot. Just seeing her would make him feel better. She was the one thing completely right in his life. He blinked, his chest tightening as he tried to focus on his diploma hanging on the wall. Margot.

She'd changed everything. Changed him. He'd followed blindly, like a child. So swept up in the sex and the adventure that he'd lost sight of his roots, of his goals. The way Edgar had looked at him, it would be a miracle if he had a job at the end of the day.

His five minutes were up. He just prayed that they liked this design, and could mark up the first presentation as a big, fat joke. Not likely.

MARGOT KNOCKED on Daniel's door, and it swung slowly open without so much as a squeak. "Daniel?"

No response, and she couldn't see him. But she did

see his jacket and portfolio on the couch. She walked through the room quickly, figuring he must have come home in a hurry.

As she approached his bedroom, she heard his voice. She couldn't make out the words, but she could tell he wasn't happy. Slowing her step, she inched closer, trying to figure out who was here, what was going on.

"…embarrassment. For heaven's sake, Daniel, what were you thinking?"

Moving closer to the door, she peeked in. There was Daniel sitting at his drafting table. Next to him was an older man, tall and lean, wearing a raincoat and tortoise-framed glasses. She could only see his profile but it was enough to tell her he was Daniel's father.

"I wasn't thinking, Dad," Daniel said, his voice low and defeated. "I screwed up. They fired me. There's nothing more to say."

Margot gasped, then pressed her hand over her mouth. Daniel was fired? Oh, God. Why? He was so good at his job. He was happy there, wasn't he?

"There's a lot more to say," his father said, talking to him as if he were a child. "What did you think you would accomplish, showing them that garbage?"

"It wasn't garbage, it was just a new idea."

"Daniel, I sent them to your firm, to you, because I trusted you. When I got that call this afternoon, I couldn't believe my ears. What's happened to you? You had to move to the city, fine. But here? With these—

"My move to Chelsea has nothing to do with it."

"No? Then maybe you can tell me what does. I can't,

in all good conscience, invite you to join my firm, you know that, don't you?"

"Yes. And I wouldn't go even if you did, so don't sweat it."

Margot heard the older man sigh. When he moved, she backed up fast and hurried through the living room and out the front door. It wasn't until she was on the stairwell that she stopped, her head pressed against the cold wall, her heart hammering in her chest. Guilt filled her until there was nothing else.

Nothing.

18

DANIEL KNOCKED on Margot's door again. She might still be at work, but it was late. Almost ten-thirty. He should have called her, but he'd been wiped out.

After his father had left, he'd just sat there. Staring at the drawings that had buried him. Edgar had been calm. He'd come into his office after the CPAs had left. Talked to him about responsibility, reputations. He'd asked if Daniel was in trouble with substance abuse. Then he'd told him that he was sorry. Very sorry. But that he had to think about the firm, the clients, and that perhaps Daniel would be happier working in a more liberal atmosphere.

So that was that. He'd been so sure. His designs weren't even that... They were wrong. He'd been wrong. Wrong to think he knew better, that he could change them. The irony was, he hadn't even known his father had sent the CPAs to him. Of course, his father would never do anything so gauche as to broadcast his favors. He'd simply assume that his son was up to the task. Now they both understood.

He knocked again, a little more loudly, and Margot's weak voice said, "Come in."

It wasn't locked. And the room was dark. He could

see her, sitting on the couch, hugging her knees, the moonlight shining in her hair while shadows obscured her face. "Margot? What's wrong?"

She sniffed as he rushed toward her, narrowly missing the side of the coffee table in the dark.

He touched her back, and she jerked away. "Babe, what is it? Are you okay?"

"I'm fine," she said, although she didn't sound fine in the least.

He sat down next to her, but his hand hovered over her, afraid to touch. "Talk to me."

"I'm sorry," she said.

He didn't think he'd heard her, she'd spoken so softly. "What?"

"I'm sorry. I messed up everything. I didn't mean to, but it doesn't matter, because it's all gone to hell and it's my fault."

"What are you talking about?"

She turned to him, and while he couldn't see her clearly, tears glistened on her cheeks. "I know what happened."

"To whom?"

"You," she said, her frustration clear. "I went to see you, and the door was open. I didn't know your father was there, or I wouldn't have come in."

"Oh."

"I heard him. He said you were fired. You tried to sell them on your personal designs, didn't you."

It wasn't a question, but he nodded anyway.

"Oh, God, Daniel. It's all my fault."

"How is it your fault? I drew them. I made the idiotic decision to show them. You had nothing to do with it."

She waved her hand at him dismissively. "Who the hell did I think I was? I'm nothing, nobody. I had no business trying to change you. You're fine, you're perfect, and I'm…"

"You're not nothing and certainly not nobody. And I do have a mind of my own."

She sniffed as her face sort of crumbled into a sob. He wanted to hold her, take it away, but when he moved closer, she pulled back. "Your clothes, your hair. I was so incredibly arrogant. You should never have moved here. Never have met me. Then you'd have your job, the life you're supposed to. Everything I touch turns to crap."

"Honey, you didn't do anything to me. I'm a big boy, I make my own decisions."

"Oh, sure. You poor sap. I could have asked you to dye your hair pink and you would have."

He winced. "Probably. And to tell you the truth, when I first got fired I put a lot of the blame on you."

Her whole body tightened, which he hadn't wanted. "I'm not finished. When I calmed down I realized things are turning out the way they should. If you did anything, it was open my eyes, that's all. It's not about blame."

She shoved him, not hard, just away. "Yes, it is. Damn it, Daniel, you were doing all this wonderful stuff to please me, which meant so—" She sniffed again. "But I wasn't doing you any favors. When I told you I loved your private designs, I meant it, but I never meant for you to—"

"Stop it, okay? I don't know how else to say it's not your fault."

She sighed with such weariness, then looked to her

left, to the window. "I just don't think it's such a good idea for us to see each other anymore."

He couldn't believe what he heard. Wouldn't. "Margot, don't be—"

"I'm losing it at work, too. I almost got fired myself. Isn't that a heck of a coincidence. I'm holding on by the skin of my teeth."

"And you think I'm the reason?"

She nodded slowly. "I'm not blaming you. It's just not smart for us to do this. Neither of us."

"The only thing that's worth anything to me is you."

She moaned, turned back to him. He wished he could see her eyes. "Shut up, Daniel. Just shut up and go, okay?"

"No."

"Please."

"We don't have to do this."

She breathed deeply for a long time. Letting the air go with effort. Never moving, not even sniffling. "Yes we do," she said, finally.

He didn't know what to do. She didn't mean it. She couldn't. But if she truly believed she was screwing up at work because of him, then…

"I just want you to know something, and then I'll leave. I've never felt more alive than the time we've been together. You mean a great deal to me, and the last thing on earth I'd ever want is to hurt you. But know this. You are not to blame for anything in my life, except for making me happy. For making me see who I really am."

He could see her shoulders tremble in the dim light, fresh tears snaking down to curl under her chin. He leaned over and touched her lips with his as gently as he could. Then he walked away, tasting her sorrow as he closed the door behind him.

MARGOT MADE IT TO WORK the next day, even though she'd barely slept at all. She couldn't believe what she'd done to him. To herself.

She'd just been so damn happy. So happy, she'd let this stupid Whompies job get completely out of control. And with it, her chances of making it in television. All her plans were vanishing under her fingertips because she'd fallen for Daniel. Oh, God, had she fallen. She could hardly think of him without her breath catching, without a painful ache.

But she had work to do. She'd made it through yesterday with no phone call from Janice, but that didn't mean she wouldn't get one today. And she still had no idea if they were sending her another body. It would be all right if only her fingers would obey. If she could just stop the damn crying.

"He wants an ETA."

Margot looked up from the prep table. At least today it was something simple. Chicken nuggets. She turned to the first AD. "Half an hour."

The woman left, and she got her ass in gear. All that was left was the coloring. She used maloise and each nugget had to be painted before she put it in the oven. She used her fingers, making sure each one was perfect.

After they were toasted to perfection, she placed the nuggets on a Whompies place mat, making sure the logo showed and that the chicken was placed just so.

Then she put a Whompies soft-drink cup on the tray next to a plastic ketchup packet, also with the logo visible, and headed out to see what new insults the director would come up with today.

He was moving everything. Every last morsel, cursing at her under his breath the whole time. She shrank back into the shadows, not wanting to hear it, or see his glowering face. This was it. She was officially going down the tubes, and there wasn't a thing she could do about it. They'd never want her to do TV again. Her plan was a bust, right out of the gate.

She had one more setup to do before they were done today. Nothing fancy, just a chicken salad. Although she wanted to walk out the door and never come back, she went to the prep kitchen and began. Bettina was working on the lettuce, and Rick was picking out olives. Margot set to work, taking each step as it came, working as carefully as she knew how. Lettuce, onion, tomato, shaved carrots, croutons, chicken. There was nothing she couldn't handle, nothing she hadn't done before. The outcome wasn't her business. They'd like it or not, but she would do the best she could. She wouldn't try to change Whompies, change anyone. Not ever again.

The day inched along, heartbeat by heartbeat. She took to speaking aloud, talking herself through each motion, as if she were learning the craft all over again. She didn't take a break, didn't stop for lunch. Moving as quickly as she could, she gradually saw the salad come together. She sweated over every piece of lettuce, every vegetable. After five batches, she got the perfect pieces of breaded chicken. By the time they called her on to the set, she was as ready as she'd ever be.

Walking with care, she maneuvered through the mayhem of the set and placed the tray on the long table. Ignoring everything and everyone, she designed the set, nothing escaping her attention. When she could do no more, when the last tiny shred of carrot was in position, she returned to the kitchen.

The last thing she heard before the door closed behind her was the director calling her a stupid bitch.

"DAD. I DIDN'T EXPECT to hear from you." Daniel leaned back against his couch, not at all prepared for this. The night had been about as bad as a night could be. All he'd wanted to do was to go back to Margot's, reason with her. Plead with her if need be. But the only rational part of his mind that remained convinced him to let it go. At least for right now. He wasn't exactly in the best shape, and Margot needed time to think things through. They both did.

"I have a number for you," his father said. "Are you ready?"

Daniel got a pad and pen from his side table. "Yeah."

His father gave him the number, then a name. "Alexander Arntzen. The firm isn't in the same league as Kogen, but Arntzen is willing to give you a chance."

Daniel closed his eyes. Put the pen down. "Thank you. I appreciate what you're doing. But I'm not going to call him."

There was a long pause where Daniel heard only the sound of his father's breathing. Finally, "Why not?"

"Because I'm going in another direction, Dad. I don't want to work for Arntzen."

"But you don't know anything about his firm."

"It's one you like. Respect."

"And that automatically means it's worthy of your disdain."

"Not at all. I'm sure they do very commendable work. I know your taste, Dad. I tried to have your taste, your ideas. But it didn't work out very well."

"You're being ridiculous."

"I'm being honest. I want to work somewhere I can stretch. Somewhere they're interested in the future, not the past."

"Trends come and go, boy. It's the traditions that stay. That keep going year after year. That's what has kept me in business. Don't be rash about this, Daniel. I raised you better than that."

"You did a fine job, Dad. But I'm going to do this my way."

"All right," his father said, and then he hung up.

Daniel turned off his phone, and put it in the charger. He tore off the sheet of paper and crumpled it in his hand. When he went to the kitchen to get some coffee, he tossed it in the trash.

He hadn't enjoyed upsetting his father, but this was too important to cave in. Despite the consequences of his actions, yesterday had been a revelation to him. He'd never felt that kind of excitement at his work before. Even doing his private fantasy designs hadn't given him that kind of…exhilaration. It was a feeling he'd never even expected in connection with work.

A quiet satisfaction, yes. But not that.

Margot was right. She had changed him. Given him a whole new life, and it had nothing to do with style or haircuts or even great sex. It was all about options. Being willing. Opening himself to new experiences and ideas.

The truth was, he couldn't have stayed working for Edgar. Not after yesterday. They'd given him a very decent termination package, and with his savings, he wasn't in a panic to find a new job. He'd take his time. Find a firm that wanted the kind of ideas he had. That wouldn't put him in the kind of constricting box that had atrophied his creative muscles for so long.

He fixed his coffee, then went to the living room. This actually would have been a good day. A new beginning. But the one person who would really understand, who he wanted desperately to tell, didn't want to see him.

He'd had no idea Margot was having such problems at her own work. She'd said nothing to him. No, that's not true, she'd told him the director was an ass, and that it wasn't as easy as print work. But she'd hidden any real issues. Was that the problem then? Did she feel she couldn't talk to him about that kind of thing?

God, he was a selfish bastard. He should have asked more questions, probed more deeply into what was going on in her life. It was always about him, wasn't it? Shit, he was more like his mother than he thought. The idea was repugnant. Margot made it so easy. Took care of him, without ever making him feel smothered or trapped..

He looked into the future of his days and especially

his nights, and the prospect of no Margot made his chest constrict. Before Chelsea, before her, it had all been the motions, and he hadn't even seen. He'd accepted so much mediocrity. It was as if he'd been in the middle of a swamp, sinking down a little more each day. Taking one more assignment that didn't challenge him, going on one more date that left him feeling tired. Compromise followed compromise with nothing to show him that he was in the swamp at all.

And then he'd moved, and there was Margot and the dinners, Devon and Eric, knit scarves and caps, even the drama of Corrie. Everything new and alive and nothing pulling him down except the work. And she'd shown him the way out of that swamp, too. The way she'd looked at him when he'd shared his secret had made him strong. Given him new eyes.

He couldn't go back now. How could he when he understood that the swamp was just over there, a footstep away. He needed to be on guard, to try the things that scared him, to make love to the woman who wanted him to be the man he should be.

That wasn't smart. He shouldn't have thought about making love to her. Not now, when he couldn't have her. She'd become…

Friendship and sex. That's what she'd offered him. It's what she'd given him. Given him so generously, and he'd taken everything she had offered.

He wanted her back. He just had no idea what to do about it.

19

MARGOT PRESSED THE BUTTON on her answering machine, cutting off Daniel's plea before she'd heard it all. Listening to his voice hurt too much. Knowing what she'd done, how she'd manipulated him. Because she could. Because she always had.

She'd actually thought it was charming. That people liked her because of her bold ideas and her pushy ways. But once she'd looked at her life without the rose-colored glasses, she could see that she'd caused an incredible amount of havoc in her wake.

As far back as grade school, she'd been playing God. Making her friends dress in what pleased Margot, giving unasked-for advice, shunning those who dared disobey. She'd been insufferable, but she'd kept those who didn't think for themselves close at hand so she never had to look. To take responsibility.

It hadn't gotten better over the years. In fact, she'd gotten worse. She was so happy to be here, in this building, because everyone here tolerated her bad behavior. They were like her, wanting to change the world to fit their specifications.

What a team.

And poor Daniel hadn't stood a chance. For whatever

reason, he'd wanted her, and the chemistry between them was undeniable. He'd wanted her, and that made him moldable. And mold she had.

She'd stripped him of more than his wardrobe. Cut off a lot more than hair. And she'd thought it was fun. That she was helping.

She crumpled onto her couch. How could there be more tears? She should be drained, dry, and yet they came. Five days. Five days and four nights of crying her heart out. But even if the tears never ended, it didn't matter. She had work to do. Now. Even when Daniel was just a few steps away, wanting—

She pulled out her laptop and booted up. First, she owed the ladies at Eve's Apple a horribly truthful letter. An update on her Man To Do. Her Man She'd Done Wrong.

She went to her e-mail and started typing, letting it out. All of it. Telling her story without any omissions, letting them know exactly who she was, and how she'd screwed up. It took a long time, and she praised spell check because she'd made as many mistakes in her note as she had with Daniel.

Before she had a chance to edit, to make herself look better, she sent it off. Bully for her, but wasn't confession supposed to be good for the soul? Or something?

A break for a new box of tissues, a nose blow, and then the real task of the morning: Margot's future.

She titled the page, dated it. Then she began with a list of the things that had gone wrong on the Whompies job. It was long. Just when she was going to get her favorite paring knife to slit her wrists, she started her second list. What she'd done right. At first, she couldn't think of anything more than being on time and good hygiene. But she forced herself to sit there, sipping coffee, computer on her lap, and slowly the good started to reveal itself.

She'd been working her butt off, but the shoots had been ridiculously understaffed, leaving her to take up the slack. The assistants they did have were clueless. Even though the kitchen was fabulous, when she had to explain every detail five times, it kind of lost its charm. The director was an ass of the first order, and he hadn't given her any direction, just criticism.

Which didn't mean squat. She should have been able to handle it. Demanded better help. More experienced help. She should have confronted the director early on, let him know what she needed, convinced him they could be a team.

It wasn't her styling skills that sucked, it was her management skills. She'd been an assistant on so many shoots, she should have learned more. Granted, none of them had been this hellish, but still. She'd hadn't been proactive in the least. She'd let the situation get the better of her, instead of owning it. Owning her strengths, and her weaknesses.

She picked up her coffee and it was stone cold. No wonder. She'd been at this for hours. She should get showered, dress. Face the day. Make some decisions.

See Daniel.

Only, she couldn't, could she?

Missing someone shouldn't hurt this much. It hadn't been like this with Gordon. She'd been miserable, sure, but this was like a part of her had been amputated without anesthetic.

But what could she do?

She opened a new page on her computer. She labeled this page What Went Wrong with Daniel:

1. She'd presumed to know the man when she didn't know him at all.
2. She arrogantly went about changing him from the outside in, with no thought to the consequences.
3. She used sex to manipulate him. She'd promised friendship and sex and then, like a fool, she'd fallen in love. Deeply in love. So in love that the thought of being without him made her physically ill.

Not a terribly long list, but long enough to have completely screwed up two lives. Good for her. Short and sweet. No messy ambiguities to get in the way.

"Enough," she said aloud, changing to page two.

What Went Right:

1. She'd been given friendship and sex. The best of both. Friendship she'd never dreamed of having with a guy, especially a straight guy. Sex that not only broke all the laws of physics, but had changed the very makeup of her heart. A separate entity from anything she'd known, anything she'd dreamed. Being with Daniel was like…

Okay, enough of number one.

2. She'd made him feel welcome. Minutes before she'd seduced him.
3. He'd been incredible with her family. Which was a big honkin' deal.
4. He looked a lot better.

Wait, was that a right or a wrong?

5. She'd never been happier. Not ever. Even with the work debacle, she'd been…truly, madly, deeply happy.
6. She loved him.
7. She loved him.
8. She loved him.

Oh, God.

DEVON NODDED toward the couch. "Sit. I'll bring drinks."

Daniel had been in Devon and Eric's apartment before as part of the traveling Sunday dinners, but it still surprised him. It was normal. An apartment. Nice furniture, nice artwork. Nice. Not a naked cherub in sight.

"I've got beer and schnapps," Devon said from the kitchen.

"Beer's great, thanks."

Just as Devon was coming back, Eric came out from the bedroom. "Hey, Daniel." He was dressed in worn jeans, a pale blue T-shirt, barefoot. Even Daniel, who was terminally hetero, could see why some men might find him attractive. He and Devon, who was similarly clad in jeans and T.

Eric sat down on the other end of the couch while Devon gave Daniel his beer, then took a seat across the way.

Daniel cleared his throat, then took a big drink of the beer, which was cold and great, despite the fact that it was just after five. Normally he didn't drink this early, but he didn't care.

"So what the hell's going on with Margot?" Eric asked.

"I was hoping you'd tell me."

"We don't know anything that happens in this building."

"No?"

"Well, not this time, at least," Devon said. "Which is actually pretty upsetting. You really messed things up, huh?"

Daniel gave Devon his most acerbic glare.

Eric leaned forward, also hitting Devon with a cutting glance. "What the charmer here is saying is that this thing between you two has obviously torn her up. I can see you're not doing too well, yourself."

Daniel looked down at his clothes. He was in chinos and a shirt, no different from most other days. But if he looked like he felt, it must be pretty bad. "So what now?"

"I assume you've tried to talk to her?"

"She won't answer the door or her phone. All she said to me was that me losing my job was all her fault. Which is absurd."

Eric and Devon exchanged a look that told him there was more to this than he knew.

"What?"

"Come on. You know Margot."

He leaned back as the air left his lungs. "No," he said, the reality hitting him smack in the face. "I don't. I know where she grew up, a few things about her family. But not really. We, uh, mostly talked about me." The admission was hard.

"She's always been like this, Daniel," Eric said. "She's the ultimate party planner, but she goes a lot deeper."

"You're going to have to translate that into something I can understand."

Devon smiled at him. "Margot likes to jump in the mix. With people, mostly. She has these ideas about how people should look, how they should dress, how they should decorate. Who they should be. And the weird thing about it is that she's right almost all the time."

Eric went on. "She has a remarkable gift. She doesn't just work her magic with food. She does it with people. She could teach all those yahoos on *Queer Eye for the Straight Guy* how to really do their thing. Seriously, I've never met anyone with a keener sense of individual style. We all play with her, 'cause, well, we have no lives, but she's the queen."

"Like what she did about my clothes. My haircut."

"Yeah. And I'm thinking," Eric said, "that this time she believes she's gone too far."

"But she hasn't. She's right. She has changed things in my life, but I don't mind. I like it."

"Did you tell her?"

He nodded. "Not just once."

"Still, she believes you lost your job because of what she did."

Daniel sighed. "Yeah. Thing is, I would have quit anyway. I want more. But I also know things weren't going well with her at work. She said it was because of us."

"Did she say why?"

He shook his head. "Maybe I distracted her too much."

"Well," Devon said, leaning back and spreading his arms expansively. "One thing seems very clear. She's full of crap."

Daniel couldn't help but laugh.

"It's true. I've never seen her happier. Daniel, you need to go have a serious talk with that woman, and shake some sense into her. I love her to death, but I swear, sometimes she can be such a moron."

Still smiling, Daniel shook his head. "She's the farthest thing from a moron I know." He stared past Devon's head to the abstract painting on the opposite wall. It was full of red and purple and yellow, vivid colors, totally alive. "She's amazing. When I'm with her, I'm better. Brighter. I've never met a living soul like her, and doubt I ever will again. I don't want to blow this, gentlemen. And I'm ashamed to admit the fact that when it comes to women, I'm the moron."

"Go over there, Daniel." Eric stood up. "Go."

"She won't—"

"She will. Trust me. Just go."

MARGOT HAD GOTTEN through the shower. She'd even gotten dressed, although she wished now she had just put on some jeans. But the intention was to look nice. Because she needed something nice. The makeup was part of it, but it was also a last-ditch attempt to stem the flood of tears. It had been a dismal failure.

She swiped the bottom of her eyes again and came away with black gunk. Damn. She walked over to her coffee table where she'd printed out all her lists and spread them around like puzzle pieces.

At least she felt a little better about the work thing. It wasn't easy to look at her own failings, but the alternative was worse. If she didn't look, she couldn't fix. And she wasn't about to crawl into a hole about this.

Her whole life was on the line. Whatever shell of a life she had left. If she couldn't have Daniel, at least she could salvage what was left of her career. She'd regroup, that's all. She'd written a killer speech, one that she intended to memorize and give to Janice tomorrow. And if Janice still wanted to can her, so be it. She'd find another TV gig, because damn it, she could do it.

And if she found herself in another situation with no help and a horrifying boss, she'd take immediate steps, and not let her own fear and insecurity rule the day. She'd faced adversity before. She wasn't born a stylist, right? Right. She could do it. She could make it. She could.

She was so totally screwed.

Why'd she have to do that to him? He was supposed to be for sex, that's all. Sex and fun and dressing up like a big Ken doll. A Man to Do. She wasn't supposed to fall in love with the guy.

The phone rang, but she already knew who it was,

and she wasn't going to answer. If she did, if she spoke to him for even a second, it would all be over. And she couldn't do that to Daniel. Not Daniel.

He deserved a life sans her interference. Sans Margot altogether.

It rang four times and then the machine answered. It wasn't Daniel. It was Corrie.

"Margot? Honey? Open the door. Okay? We love you."

That was it. The whole message. Why would Corrie call her to—

Oh.

She waited for it. Counted to three.

The knock came. Soft. Tentative. Then his voice.

"Margot?"

She closed her eyes, pressing them with the backs of her fingers.

"Margot, please, can we just talk? I think we need to talk."

The phone rang again, and this time it was Eric.

"Margot, don't be an ass. He's the best thing that's ever happened to you. Open the door."

She shook her head, stood up. She'd go to the bedroom. Shut the door. Unplug the phone.

"Margot?"

"Go away, Daniel," she said, only so softly it was more of a wish than a command.

"I miss you. And I don't blame you. I would have quit that job anyway. I swear to God. I shouldn't have been working there, but I didn't see, okay? I didn't get it until you. Until you believed in me."

"Stop," she said, just a bit louder.

She hardly noticed the phone ringing again, or Devon's voice telling her to open the damn door, that they had all night, and they weren't going to give up.

"It's like this, Margot," Daniel said, and she could picture him. With his short, dark hair. His incredible blue eyes. The lines that were dimples only longer on the sides of his face that she loved to lick. His lips, so soft, and full and oh, this wasn't fair.

So why couldn't she move? It wasn't that far to the bedroom. To the bathroom where she could lock the door, turn on the radio and play it really loud.

"I've been thinking about this a lot," he said, his voice muffled through the door, but still, it was his voice and it made her melt, "…and I know what I did wrong. I didn't… I wasn't there for you. I didn't ask about your work. I should have known you were in trouble. Anyone who wasn't so selfish would have seen it. I just was so… Margot, I'm sorry. I mean it. I never meant to hurt you. And I was an idiot, and it's my fault. Not yours. You've done nothing wrong, Margot."

The phone rang again, and she couldn't stand it one more second. She grabbed it and yanked out the damn battery, and threw it on the couch with all her might. But the answering machine answered anyway.

"*Bubele?* Call your mother."

Margot's chin fell onto her chest. Her life just couldn't get any more twisted.

Another knock, and this one was stronger. "Margot, please. Just open the door. Because there's something really important I have to tell you and I don't want to say it to wood."

She turned, her tummy full of butterflies, her heart not daring to hope. And her foot moved toward him. The other foot followed, and then she was there, standing inches from the man on the other side. He wanted to tell her something important, and her head, no matter how forcefully she screamed that it couldn't be so, insisted that what he wanted to tell her was the thing she wanted to hear more than anything on earth.

Her hand went to the knob, and saying the fastest and most heartfelt prayer in the world, she opened the door.

20

THE MOMENT SHE SAW HIM, she crumbled. Not on the floor, or even with her face. But inside, everything fell apart. The list of What Went Wrong with Daniel ran through her head, her mistakes in bold type followed by huge exclamation points.

She knew what she had to do.

Instead, she turned, and walked through the living room. At first, she thought he wouldn't follow, then she heard his footsteps. The softest whisper behind her. He said her name, and derailed the last bit of sense in her body.

As she reached her bedroom door, her steps slowed, but her insanity didn't waver. She couldn't stop this. Just once more, she needed to feel his body next to hers. To look into that incredible face and pretend…

She went to her bed and turned to find him standing by her door.

"Margot."

She lifted her dress over her head and tossed it on the chair.

"Honey, we need to talk."

But she didn't want to talk. To talk would mean to tell the truth. She reached behind her back, unclasping her bra. She let if fall from her body, barely aware of the material hitting her toes.

He struggled to keep his gaze on her face, but he couldn't. He looked down, at her naked breasts. And when she put her thumbs under the edge of her panties, he followed her all the way down, watched her step aside, slide off her mules. When she stood, he watched that, too.

She pushed her shoulders back, covered only by her tears.

He moaned, but he held perfectly still. "Wait."

"No."

"Please, Margot. I have things to say."

She moved to the bed and sat on the edge. She lifted the comforter and covered the most vulnerable parts of herself. "Okay," she said. "I'm listening."

He kept his gaze on her face. "I'm sorry."

"For what?"

"For not being your friend."

"What are you talking about?"

"I didn't know about your job, Margot. What a rough time you'd been having. I didn't know because I didn't ask. I should have."

"You did. I didn't want to talk about it."

"And being the *mensch* I was, I didn't press. I should have. It wasn't fair and it wasn't right, and I'm so sorry."

She turned her head, wiped her cheek. "It wasn't—"

"If you say it wasn't my fault…"

She sniffed. "You'll what?"

He didn't answer her. When she turned back to see why, he was standing right next to her. When she lifted her gaze to his, he touched the curve of her neck, brushed his thumb over her cheekbone while his eyes traced every corner of her face.

Margot pressed her cheek into his palm, unable to look away. Only when he leaned in to kiss her did her eyes flicker shut.

Daniel's lips barely touched hers at first, his breath slipping into her body. Then he traced her lips with the tip of his tongue, making her quiver all the way to her toes. She moaned and it felt like surrender. Daniel's grip tightened and he sealed his mouth over hers in a deep, hungry kiss, his languid tongue teasing hers, reaching everywhere, claiming her.

His hands ran up and down her back, touching her as if he'd never felt her before, his desperation clear in his shaking fingers, in his kiss.

He pulled back to meet her gaze. A tear made its way down her cheek, and he captured it with the pad of his finger. "Thank you," he whispered. "For so much."

She stood and reached for the buttons on his shirt. "Please," was all he could say.

He stopped her hand, moved it away. Then he took over. There was no finesse, no sensual striptease, but his eyes kept her glued to the spot, watching breathlessly as he removed his shirt, his pants. Toed off his shoes and his socks.

There they were, standing close enough to share their heat. Their desire. When he breached the distance and touched her cheek, she was lost.

She fell and the bed was there to catch her. His hard body half covered hers, and his warmth melted something she hadn't known was frozen. When he kissed her, took her mouth in a savage embrace, she abandoned herself to the pleasure of him. For this perfect moment, there was nothing else. No failure, no regrets, no heartache. Just his hands and his chest and the hot erection against her thigh. She needed to feel him inside her. She needed…

Daniel ran his tongue down the side of her jaw, lower to the hollow of her neck. He wanted to taste every part of her. Her body beneath his fingers was alive—tense and expectant. Incredibly responsive. She moaned as his lips found her nipple and he sucked and licked and pulled. Teased the tiny ring there.

He licked across the distance to her other nipple which was beaded and warm, perfect in his mouth. His skin against hers, the softness addictive, the scent of her imprinted deeply in the pleasure center of his brain.

He moved down, nipping at the flesh of her stomach, then comforting the hurt with the flat of his tongue. He rubbed his cheek against the soft rise of her belly then drifted slowly down. She spread her legs, making room for his shoulders, and then he kissed the very edge of her lower lips, breathing in her musky sweetness before carefully running his tongue down as far as he could go.

She moaned again, lifting her hips in invitation. He accepted greedily, and when he tasted the wet heat, he had to lift himself from the friction of the bed so he wouldn't come.

Beneath him, she bucked and twisted, her hand gripping his hair painfully, but he didn't care at all. He knew how to please her and he would be relentless.

As Margot remembered how to breathe again, she made her fingers work enough to pull Daniel up into her arms. He wiped her cheeks, and smiled at her as if he'd just done the most fantastic magic trick. Which he had.

She'd never felt anything so powerful, more incredible. And still she wanted more. She wanted him inside her. "Please," she said again.

He grew serious and she felt his body tense. Slowly, as if he could break her, he shifted until he was over her, his arms taking most of his weight.

She felt him between her thighs, his thick length brushing her flesh.

He smiled again only this time there was something in the flash of his blue eyes. Something predatory. He spread her knees with his own, and brought himself to her entrance. As he thrust inside her, he whispered, "Mine."

She breathed in the hint of spices from his hair as he settled back into the cradle of her arms. They were still breathing harshly, but her own personal hero had maneuvered the covers over them so they were safe and warm. His hand rested on her breast, not teasing or anything, just comfortably resting. As if he belonged there.

"Margot?"

He spoke softly, asking permission. It was time. Whatever happened from here, she could handle it. She only wished the spark of hope in her heart wasn't quite so strong. "Daniel."

He shifted again, this time sitting up enough so he could see her face. She scooted back to rest against the pillows. Although he wasn't touching her breast, he'd taken her hand in his. "So what the hell happened?"

"Uh, we had sex."

"Before that."

"Oh. That."

"Yeah."

She swallowed, looked away.

His fingers touched her beneath her chin, and brought her gaze back to meet his. "No cheating."

"Okay."

"Again, what happened?"

"It all kind of went to hell."

"How?"

"You lost your job."

He nodded. "And?"

"I did it."

"I was under the impression that my boss fired me."

"He did it because—"

"Because I presented a design that was completely wrong for the clients."

"Because—"

"Because I realized I didn't want to design buildings for old fogeys any more."

"B—"

"Because you helped me see that I was more than that. That I want more."

"I meddled."

He nodded.

"I stuck my nose where it didn't belong."

"Fair enough, at least in the beginning."

"Meaning?"

"Your nose became pretty welcome. Uh, that didn't come out right."

She couldn't help but laugh at the way his face scrunched up. But her laughter died a quick death as she remembered her long list. "I made presumptions I had no right to make. I was arrogant and stupid, and I never once considered the consequences."

"Wow, that's pretty bad."

She nodded. "I know."

"What else?"

"You need more?"

He nodded. "Everything. Every last horrible detail."

She sat up straighter, knowing he deserved this, and more. "I used sex to get what I wanted."

He frowned, and that crinkle between his eyebrows deepened. "When?"

"Every time."

"You mean, when we went to the art gallery?"

She nodded, hot fresh tears burning her eyes.

"When I climbed into the shower and took you from behind?"

She nodded again, despite the shiver that went up her spine.

He leaned closer. "When you got between my legs after you cut my hair."

She buried her head in her hands. "Oh, God."

He touched her gently on the arm. "Come on. We're not through."

Sniffing, she faced him again. So ashamed.

"And you say that you used this sex that we had to get what you wanted."

"Uh-huh."

"Which was…?"

"What?"

"What nefarious thing did you want that you had to ply me with sex to get?"

"You."

The corners of his lips moved, but just for a moment. And if she wasn't mistaken, that was humor making his forehead rise.

"It's not funny."

"Absolutely not."

"I'm serious, Daniel. I was selfish and inconsiderate and I just took and took and…"

"And I was helpless the whole time? Caught in your spell? Totally unable to think for myself, to make my own decisions, because sex with you stopped all functioning above the waist?"

She opened her mouth, but nothing came out. When he said it like that… "I promised friendship and sex," she said, her voice low and her gaze somewhere in the middle of his chest.

"Oh, that."

She nodded miserably.

"You didn't lie. That's what I got. Friendship and sex. Great sex. Great friendship. Who could ask for anything more?"

Her heart sank to her toes. Hope fled, leaving her utterly empty.

"I mean," he went on, as if he hadn't just destroyed her life, "if it wasn't for all that friendship and all that sex, I probably wouldn't have fallen in love with you."

Margot blinked, not trusting that she'd heard what she'd thought… "What?" She looked up again, into his eyes.

"I said, I probably wouldn't have fallen in love with you."

"Oh."

He leaned in. "Is that all you have to say?"

She shook her head.

He laughed. "Well?"

She opened her mouth. Shut it again. Then the synapses fired somewhere deep inside and she knew he was telling her the truth, that despite her best meddling, her foolish promises, he really did love her. "I love you, too."

"Yeah?"

She nodded.

"Hmm, doesn't sound like you're very enthusiastic about it."

"I am."

"Oh?"

She smiled slowly. "So you want proof, huh?"

"It might help. After all, we've already determined that I'm not the brightest bulb in the chandelier."

"Are you kidding?"

He shook his head. "You're the one who said it. Not me."

"I did not. I think you're brilliant and talented, and funny and sweet and you can do anything in the—" She closed her mouth. "Oh."

"Exactly."

"So I didn't…"

He put his hands on the sides of her face and shook her gently. "No, you didn't." Then he pulled her close.

Just before their lips touched, she whispered, "You want proof? I'll give you proof."

"I don't convince easily, you know."

"Don't worry. I have my ways."

"I know you do, Margot. And for the record, I'm crazy about your ways."

Epilogue

Six Months Later...

"MA, I CAN'T TALK NOW. Daniel's gonna be home any minute."

"So, you have to hang up on your own mother?"

"It's a really big day, Ma. He made his first presentation at the new firm."

"What are you worried about? You tell me all the time he's a genius."

"He is."

"So?"

"So, we're going to celebrate."

"*Oy.* What else is new?"

Margot smiled, thinking about the amount of champagne they'd had in the past few months. There was the night he'd moved in with her. The day she'd gotten her second commercial gig with Galloway and Donnelly, the bottle of Cristal when the shoot ended and the director had given her a dozen red roses and requested her for all his future projects. Then Daniel had gotten his new job, which he loved. "Yeah, we're just celebrating fools," she said, liking the sound of it.

"All right, I give up. Call me tomorrow."

"I will, Ma. Say hi to Dad."

"Don't get me started."

Margot laughed as she clicked off the phone. It was almost time, and she hurried into the kitchen to pull the bubbly out of the fridge. The two flutes were already on the table. She opened the bottle, the pop an incredibly satisfying sound. As she poured the first glass, she heard the key in the door.

Then he was there, standing in what used to be her apartment, now theirs, with a much more eclectic mix of styles and a whole new feel. She shivered as she looked at him. It didn't seem to matter if she'd seen him eight hours ago or ten minutes, he just made her melt.

"Who," Daniel said, throwing his jacket and briefcase in the direction of the couch, "is gifted, talented and an architect ahead of his time?"

"Um, Frank Lloyd Wright?"

"Close," he said, approaching her slowly. "But no cigar."

She smiled. "You."

He nodded.

"They loved it."

He walked toward her and she could see the satisfaction and happiness in his eyes, the bounce in his step. "They went crazy. Called the design brilliant."

He got close, but instead of reaching for the champagne he reached for her.

She put down the glasses and curled into his arms. "The designer is brilliant."

He sighed into her hair. "Yeah, I am."

She laughed. "Modest, too."

He kissed her, deeply, slowly. And when he finally pulled back he looked at her in that way of his. With love and excitement right there. "I have an idea," he said.

"Oh?"

"I was thinking about Estelle."

"My cousin Estelle?"

He nodded. "Yeah."

"That's kinky, even for you."

He grinned. "I was thinking the orchestra at her wedding was pretty good."

Margot's heart started beating. Fast. "Okay…"

"And I was thinking, maybe we could hire them."

"For?"

"Come on, gorgeous. Make the connection."

"You want to get married?"

He nodded.

"To me?"

"No. To your aunt Sadie."

Margot could hardly breathe. She opened her mouth, but nothing came out.

"Well?" he whispered. "Will you marry me, Margot? Be my life partner? My wife?"

"Friendship," she whispered. "Sex."

"All that," he said, leaning down close. "And so much more. I love you." His lips touched hers.

"I love you back," she said, and then there were no more words.

HARLEQUIN® *Blaze*™

Sometimes the biggest mistakes are the best ones....

"I, Denise Cooke, take thee, Redford DeMoss, to be my lawful husband...." No, wait...I did that already—three years ago in a Vegas chapel after one too many Long Island Iced Teas. I married a hunky U.S. Marine I'd met only hours before. (The uniform did it.) The wedding night—week— was spectacular. Then Redford went back to the Gulf. And I went back to my real life as a New York City financial planner...and filed for an annulment.

I'm dating Barry the stockbroker these days, but I think about Redford...a lot. And now, thanks to an upcoming IRS audit, I'm about to see ex-husband again. So why am I flustered? He's probably married, and I have—um, what's his name. It's not as if Redford plans to take me back...or take me— gulp—to bed. Besides, I'd never make the same mistake twice. Not even my favorite one...

#169 MY FAVORITE MISTAKE
by Stephanie Bond

Available in February wherever Harlequin books are sold.

The world's bestselling romance series.

HARLEQUIN®
Presents~

Seduction and Passion Guaranteed!

FROM BOARDROOM
TO BEDROOM

**Harlequin Presents® brings you two
original stories guaranteed to make
your Valentine's Day extra special!**

THE BOSS'S
MARRIAGE ARRANGEMENT
by *Penny Jordan*

Pretending to be her boss's mistress is one thing—but now
everyone in the office thinks Harriet is Matthew Cole's
fiancée! Harriet has to keep reminding herself it's all just
for convenience, but how far is Matthew prepared to go
with the arrangement—marriage?

HIS DARLING VALENTINE
by *Carole Mortimer*

It's Valentine's Day, but Tazzy Darling doesn't care.
Until a secret admirer starts bombarding her with gifts!
Any woman would be delighted—but not Tazzy. There's
only one man she wants to be sending her love tokens, and
that's her boss, Ross Valentine. And her secret admirer
couldn't possibly be Ross...could it?

The way to a man's heart...is through the bedroom

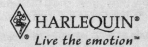

Silhouette®

Desire®

Don't miss the next story in

Dixie Browning's
new miniseries

DIVAS WHO DISH
These three friends can dish it out, but can they take it?

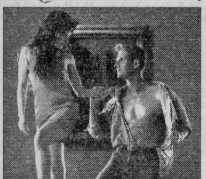

HER MAN UPSTAIRS
Available February 2005
(Silhouette Desire #1634)

Sparks flew when laid-back carpenter Cole Stevens
met his beautiful and feisty new boss, Marty Owens.
She was instantly attracted to Cole, but knew that the
higher she flew the harder she'd fall. Could her heart
handle falling for the man upstairs?

Available at your favorite retail outlet.